Cherry Pie
and Other
Stories

Elisabeth Stevens

Lite Circle Books
Baltimore, Maryland

ACKNOWLEDGEMENTS

"Campfire"—*Lite: Baltimore's Literary Newspaper:* First Prize for Fiction, 1995 Literary Contest; "The Neighbors"—*Crosscurrents;* "In The Dust"—*Farmers Market* and *Maryland Poetry Review:* First Prize, Second Annual Fiction Contest; "Wally and the Waltz"—*Monocacy Review;* "Van," "A Matter of Money," and "The Nurse —*Confrontation;* "His Ambition"—*Confrontation*: Pushcart Prize nominee; "A Rough Ride"—*Antietam Review*: Honorable Mention, 1996; "Cherry Pie"—*The Arden;* "Crumbs"—*Wind;* "The Towers"—*Playgirl.*

Copyright 2001 Elisabeth Stevens

Published September 2001 by Lite Circle Books
     P.O. Box 26162 Baltimore, MD 21210
     http://www.litecircle.com

Cherry Pie and Other Stories/Elisabeth Stevens

ISBN 0-9641622-3-7

Printed in the United States of America

In Memory of

Edward Alexander Dietrich

(1934-2001)

Contents

Cherry Pie —————————————————

Foreword

by Nancy R. Norris, Ph.D.

"How easy it is to lose what you want most!" exclaims the five-year-old protagonist in the opening story of Elisabeth Stevens' latest collection of fiction, *Cherry Pie and Other Stories*. One might well argue that all twelve stories focus on various kinds of loss—from the illusion that grown-ups always know best to the innocence that one always tells the truth. Stevens imbues her stories with the same meticulous attention to diction, cadence, and metaphor that characterizes her poetry and novels.

Indeed *Cherry Pie* demands to be read novelistically, at one sitting if possible, since it chronicles the development of a female protagonist—usually with different names—from childhood through young motherhood. The first five stories, narrated by adults who nevertheless capture the perspective of pre-pubescence, remind us of the double vision of William Faulkner's "That Evening Sun" and the opening section of James Joyce's *The Portrait of an Artist as a Young Man*. Stevens' "Campfire" and "Wally and the Waltz," in particular, gently but poignantly recreate a world of children worried about money, bullied by older children, and confused by sexuality.

The middle section of stories portrays college-age women with rich allusions to art as well as literature—certainly appropriate for an author who has illustrated many of her own stories and poems. "A Rough Ride," for example, begins: "Is it possible that a story can have a *color*? If so, this remembrance is Burnt Siena, a harsh, excremental hue I've never liked. Naples Yellow, not so far away on the color chart, has a mellow, even-aristocratic, after-sunset glow...."

The third and final section of the book brings the female

7

protagonists into young adulthood, as they cope with careers, affairs, and marriage. "The Nurse," the last story and the only one narrated from a third-person point of view, concludes in a way that also seems to interpret and integrate the sense of loss in the earlier stories. Thinking of the departure of her baby's nurse, the mother of the story realizes that "she too would lose the baby eventually—not to another nurse—but because the baby would no longer be a baby. However, that was like all the natural separations of life—inevitable as the withering of a leaf from a branch. One said good-bye to first love, first youth, children—and eventually, to life itself."

Like another American poet before her, Elisabeth Stevens brings to her understanding of loss the requisite irony that marks the opening line of Elizabeth Bishop's poem "One Art": "The art of losing isn't hard to master." Stevens' artistic treatment of loss is the readers' gain.

Campfire

How easy it is to lose what you want most! I was five; in the midst of a sheltered childhood, but I was beginning to see.

Away from home for the first time, I was the youngest at camp on a remote Adirondack lake. The head counselors, Miss Macon and Miss Heidigger, gave me the room closest to theirs. My roommate was Sally Riverton. She was six.

All summer, my mother had been sick. My father drove me upstate to the woods. When he was little, he had gone to the woods himself. Before he left me with Miss Heidigger, who was thin, and Miss Macon, who wasn't, I started to cry. He got out a white paper package tied with red and white string. It was a jar of different-colored sour balls.

"It's for you, Lillian," he said. He lifted me up and gave me a last hug. Then he got in our green car and drove away.

Miss Heidigger and I made up my cot with white camp sheets and grey camp blankets. We unpacked my bag and put my things on the shelves in the corner of the room near my bed. The other shelves were Sally's. It was time for supper—we knew because the bugle was blowing—so we didn't open my jar of sour balls. We were saving them for afterwards. I liked Miss Heidigger even though she was grey and scrimpy-looking. As we hurried to supper, I asked her to call me the special name only my mother called me. It was Lil.

Maybe she didn't hear. We were late.. Everyone was eating when we got to Miss Heidigger's table for younger girls in the big dinning hall. Sally sat on the other side of Miss Heidigger. Sally didn't need a pillow for her chair, but Miss Heidigger got one for me and lifted me up.

"Dear little Lillian," she said, taking my hand in her white wrinkly fingers and then letting go, "you're going to sit beside me every day."

The dining hall was noisy. Everyone talked at once. I didn't ask her to call me Lil again. My feet hung down. Even with the tips of my toes, I couldn't touch the floor.

After supper, big boys and girls played kick the can. I was sleepy. Miss Heidigger and Sally and I went back through the field to the dorm. Miss Heidigger helped us get ready for bed, and we opened my sour balls. We had two apiece, then Miss Heidigger patted our pillows and tucked us in. She said to call if we needed her and snapped off the light.

The bugle was blowing again in a crying way. I shut my eyes. I wasn't going to call Miss Heidigger, but I wanted something. I wanted my mother.

The whisper scared me. Maybe I thought I was in my bed at home. The whisper said: "I want another."

I wasn't sure what Sally meant. Had she said "another" or "a mother?" I opened my eyes. In the shadows I saw Sally beside my shelf. She had my jar of sour balls in her hand.

"You had some before." I sat up.

"I want some *now*."

"You're not supposed to—" I got out of bed.

"At home, my sister lets me."

I didn't have a sister or a brother either, but my mother said I might. I knew my mother *wouldn't* let me.

"Want one?" Tiptoeing to me, Sally offered the open jar. Her cheeks were puffed out. She had a sour ball in each. I could smell them.

"I'll tell Miss Heidigger—"

"If you do, you're a tattle-tale." She gave me a mean nudge with her elbow.

"*Give me—*"

"Why should I, Lil—*ee*–an?" She waved the open jar under my nose.

Reaching from under, I wrenched the jar away. "If you do anything, " I hissed, "I'll scream.." I took the black cap from my shelf where she'd left it and screwed it on as tight as I could. I got back in my cot and put the jar under my pillow.

There was a hating silence. Sally was back in her bed. She kept quiet, I kept my hand on the jar. I could have opened it, but I didn't. There was something I wanted more than a sour ball. I wanted to go home. With my head down in the pillow, I cried a long time.

I woke up when the bugle was blowing a happy song. Sally and Ann, her friend from across the hall, were jumping on the bottom of my bed.

"We want candy! We want candy!" It was louder than a whisper. Where was Miss Heidigger?

Except for a peek, I kept my eyes shut. I pretended I was asleep. With both hands under my pillow on my jar, I kept pretending.

"She isn't asleep," Sally said.

"Let's tickle her—" Ann said.

I heard footsteps—Miss Heidigger coming down the hall from the bathroom?

Sally and Ann weren't there any more. Miss Heidigger was. She was wearing a fluffy pink bathrobe. She smelled of toothpaste. Together, we picked out what I was going to wear my first day at camp. I was going to wear jodhpurs for my first riding lesson.

Breakfast was oatmeal. When oatmeal gets cold it is the same shape as the dish—like a cake you make in the sand with a pail. Cold cereal was what my mother gave us at home.

After breakfast, we were supposed to go back and make our room neat. If Sally got back first, she would take my candy, so I whispered in Miss Heidigger's ear. "May I go back by myself?" Sally didn't hear me. Miss Heidigger nodded. I ran.

The jar was still there under my pillow. The room was empty. I took my jar and ran out the back door to where the big trees were. I picked the biggest one and scraped a hole in the needles at the bottom with a grey stone. I covered up the jar and marked the place with the stone.

As I came in the back door of the dorm, Miss Macon and Miss Heidigger were coming in the front door down the long hall. At first, they didn't see me. They were looking at papers Miss Macon had.

"Another cancellation—" Miss Heidigger said in a sad, stuffed-up-nose way, "such hard times! Sally's father lost his job, and they may lose their house."

When Miss Heidigger saw me, she gave the papers back to Miss Macon who put them in the back pocket of her trousers. Miss Macon was wearing a little black watch on her big, saggy arm, and she kept winding it.

What was a cancellation? I almost asked, but I didn't. I was afraid Miss Heidigger would ask where my sourballs were. When Sally came and Miss Heidigger was helping us make our beds, I wondered how grown-ups could lose their house. I knew how to get to my house by myself from two corners away. My father showed me.

When it was time for my riding lesson, Miss Heidigger asked a big girl named Roxanne to walk me to the ring. Miss Heidigger was busy with papers. Roxanne didn't want to—I was so little. She ran out the back door, and I had to follow. "Hurry up," was all she said.

On the trail to the riding ring, Roxanne went very fast. I couldn't keep up, and there were so many trees I wasn't sure which one was mine. I didn't ask Roxanne to call me Lil.

The trail ended at a big open place. In the middle was the riding ring with logs around it and sand inside of it. The riding counselor was Herr Schmidt. He wore a big hat. And he had named all his horses. Sadie was brown and white and gentle. She was the one I was going to ride. Chet was mean and spotted black and white. He could even bite. I was to stay away from him. Fritz and Humbert were good horses, but they were for big campers like Roxanne who could ride out of the ring on long trails back into the hills.

Herr Schmidt had a name for me too. It wasn't Lil. It was

Scats. Scats meant gem. It was a name they had in Vienna, his home. In Vienna, horses could go to school. It was a Spanish school for horses named Lipizzaners.

"Of horses," Herr Schmidt asked me, "what do you know?" I told him about pony rides in the park at home.

"Ah so, Scats, we will see." Then he lifted me way up into Sadie's saddle.

I was scared. He had to shorten the stirrups and show me how to hold the reins. The first time, he walked all the way around the ring with me and Sadie. After that, Sadie and I followed Chet and the others by ourselves.

The thing I noticed most about riding was horse smell. Horse smell was the smell of the leather saddle, the reins, the stirrups and the horses themselves. After my riding lesson, I smelled that way too. Horses just raised their tails when they went to the bathroom, and it all went down into the yellow sand of the ring where other horses walked in it. It was part of the horse smell too.

When my riding time was over, Herr Schmidt showed me how to lift my leg over the saddle with one foot in the stirrup. Back on the ground, my legs felt prickly.

I wanted to tell Herr Schmidt I liked riding, but he was talking to boys who had just come back from riding the trails with Roxanne. He was telling them how Lipizzaners learned to walk on their back legs. I knew why Herr Schmidt talked about Vienna so much. He wanted to go home. I thought his mother lived there.

After riding, Roxanne walked me to crafts. This time, she didn't walk so fast. "Schmidt said you did all right on Sadie," she told me in a nicer way than before. "When I learned to ride, I wasn't much bigger than you."

The crafts shack was back near the girl's dorm, but we didn't go through the woods again, we took the camp road. The road began at the piled up stone pillars with the wooden camp sign hanging between them. It was a tar road and it had its own smell.

"It's so hot," Roxanne said, "look." She stamped the print of her foot in the soft tar, toes pointing toward the lake.

My print didn't go as deep as Roxanne's, but I pointed my toes out the black road. How I wished I were big! Then I would whoosh between the pillars to the grey road, that led to the big road, that led to the even bigger roads that led to the street of my house. Then I would be home, where my mother was...unless I got lost.

At crafts, Miss Betty was the counselor. She was pretty. She said she would help me make a boondoggle for my mother. Sally and Ann were already making them for their mothers. Sally and Ann didn't take riding. Riding cost extra. My father told me that.

To make a boondoggle to go around your neck and hold a key or a whistle or something else, you started with the hook that would hold those things and hung it on a nail. Miss Betty put my nail down low, and I choose my boondoggle ribbons—blue and white. Miss Betty started my weaving, and if I wove the wrong way, she would take it out and weave it again. Miss Betty was nice.

When it was time to stop making boondoggles, it was time for lunch. On the way to the dining hall, Sally and Ann came up close. "Where'd you put the candy?" They wanted to know.

I wouldn't tell, so Sally tried to give me an Indian burn on my arm with her two hands, each twisting a different way. Miss Betty saw and made her stop. Miss Betty was very nice.

"Miss Betty," I said, "will you call me the name my mother calls me?"

"What is it?"

"Lil."

Miss Betty smiled, then she began to laugh—I don't know why. I began to laugh too. We were silly together.

"Come on old Lil, I'll give you a ride." Then Miss Betty gave me a bouncy-jouncy piggy back the rest of the way to lunch.

Lunch was peanut butter and jelly sandwiches. Before everyone was finished, Miss Heidigger let me go, and I ran to the back of the dorm to look for my tree. I couldn't find it. I couldn't find the grey stone either. I kept looking. I wanted a sourball very much.

Then way off behind the wrong trees, I saw Miss Betty but she didn't see me. She was playing a game with the bugle blower boy. His name was Ron. Their game was: first the bugle boy took Miss Betty's hand, then she took it back. Then he took both of her hands, but she only took one back. I didn't see who would win because Miss Betty heard me crying. She came and found me.

"What are you doing here, Lil?"

"I can't find my candy tree."

I don't think she thought it was a real tree. Miss Betty laughed and lifted me up. When she wiped my tears away, her hand was hot. She held me too tight. I wanted to get down. When she put me down, she gave me a Chiclet. My mother doesn't let me chew gum, so I put it in my pocket.

The way back to the dorm was farther than I thought. I walked between them, and sometimes they swung me by my hands. Miss Betty looked pink and happy. Ron's face was red as if he'd been blowing the bugle, but he hadn't. He taught me names of his bugle songs. The happy morning one was "Reveille." The sad night one was "Taps."

Quiet time was when you were supposed to lie on your bed after lunch and rest. At the room, Sally was already there. The clothes on my shelf were messed up. My pillow was on the floor. I knew she'd been looking for my candy. She knew I knew.

"You piggy," she said, "you ate them all." Sally made a fist, maybe she was going to hit me, but then Miss Heidigger came in with our postcards. Everyone was supposed to write a postcard home. My card was a picture of the lake and so was Sally's.

"What do you want to say to your mother and father, Lillian?" Miss Heidigger asked.

I wanted to say I missed them, but I didn't tell Miss Heidigger that. So instead my card said: "I am fine at camp. I love you." Miss Heidigger wrote it for me, but I licked the green stamp myself.

Sally wrote her own card except for the address, but after it was finished, she began to cry. It wasn't quiet crying, it was loud.

"Why is Sally crying?"

What made Miss Heidigger think I could answer? I felt sad. Was Sally crying so much about my candy? Pretty soon, I was crying too.

Maybe Miss Heidigger wanted to cry along with us, but instead she got us to stop crying by getting us into our bathing suits. It was time for swimming—everyone was going to the lake. When we came to the place the trail got sandy and went down to the beach, I heard Sally say to Miss Heidigger, "Why can't I stay another week the way I was supposed to?"

I don't think Miss Heidigger told her why, but then Sally said: "I don't want to go home."

When she said that, I felt funny in my stomach. *I* wanted to go home, but I wasn't telling anybody. I wasn't even telling myself.

In the lake, I was in the crib. The crib was for girls or boys under eight or anybody who couldn't swim. It was marked out by white ropes with white balls on them. It was a long way from the raft where it was over your head.

In the winter, my mother and I had gone for swimming lessons in a pool at home. Miss Macon, who was the swimming teacher, was surprised. She said I was "a good little swimmer." Even though my mother had been too tired in the summer to take me, I hadn't forgotten. Sally couldn't swim. I could.

That night after supper, it began to rain. Nobody could play hide and seek or kick the can. Instead, Miss Macon had all the girls come into the big living room of our dorm. She made a fire in the stone fireplace and we got to toast marshmallows. I ate a lot of marshmallows with chocolate and graham crackers because of the dinner. I don't like brown bread—the raisins in it look like ants. I don't like baked beans, either.

When the marshmallows were all gone, the counselors told stories. Miss Betty's was a story I knew. It was "Cinderella." Miss Heidigger's was a true story. It was about the lake.

A long time ago, she said, the lake wasn't there at all. Instead, there was a village. When they decided to make a lake, all the people in the village had to leave so they could let the water in. Out in the middle of the lake, if you could dive way down, you might still see the church steeple.

There were other stories, but I got sleepy. When I woke up, Miss Heidigger was in her pink bathrobe, putting me to bed. I thought about the village drowned in the lake, and I heard the bugle boy blow taps. When I woke up again, someone was crying. It wasn't Sally. Who was it? It was Miss Heidigger through the wall. She and Miss Macon were talking about "cancellations" again. "If there are other parents like Sally's father," I heard Miss Heidigger say in her high-voiced way, "We won't be able to make ends meet."

What did "making ends meet" mean? I didn't know, but it made me think of how the ropes in the crib were tied and knotted together. If the ropes didn't meet, the crib could come open and you'd be over your head without knowing.

"We've got to feed them something besides beans," Miss Heidigger cried again in a way that was so sad I almost cried myself.

I heard what might have been the creaking of the big bed Miss Heidigger and Miss Macon had. Then Miss Macon talked in a voice so low I couldn't hear what she was saying. After a while, Miss Heidigger stopped crying, and I went to sleep.

Most of the week at camp was like the first day. Riding and

17

crafts in the morning. Swimming in the afternoon. I finished my mother's blue and white boondoggle with only a few mistakes. I started one for my father—red and white. I was learning the backstroke, but I was still in the crib. I looked for my sourballs, but I didn't find them.

On Wednesday, Sally got a letter from her mother on blue paper. It said they were moving. On Thursday, Roxanne got a postcard from her big brother who was in the Navy. It was a picture of the Empire State Building.

Friday came, but there wasn't any mail for me. That night we didn't have to eat beans, we had hot dogs. I like hot dogs, but I couldn't eat mine. I wanted a letter from my mother so much. Saturday, I thought my mother hadn't written because she was sick. Was she lost somewhere? Was my postcard lost in some place like the drowned village?

Saturday was different. In the morning, you could do what you wanted. No riding, no crafts, just swimming in the afternoon. After supper came the campfire. The campers leaving on Sunday got to float their candles out onto the lake. The candles were white and stuck into flat pieces of wood. Sometimes one would go a long way before it fell over into the water or got lost in the dark. Before campers got their candles, everyone stood in a big circle holding hands and sang: "Now is the hour, for me to day good-bye." Before that, Wakonda lit the campfire.

At first I didn't know who Wakonda was. Then Miss Heidigger told me he was an Indian. He was a boys' counselor, but not all the time. He didn't live at camp.

Before Wakonda's campfire began, everyone in the whole camp sat down in a circle by the lake. It was almost dark, but Miss Heidigger sat next to me and we had our flashlights. Then Wakonda came down from the bluff with an Indian blanket around him and a feather on his head. He wore Indian moccasin slippers and Indian leather trousers. When he got to the center of the circle where there were sticks standing up in a teepee way, we were very quiet.

From his belt, which was a tied piece of leather, Wakonda took two sticks. One was pointed, the other had a place where you put the point. With a little piece of leather he had, Wakonda made the pointed stick turn back and forth. He did that for such a long time that I got tired. Then it happened. There was smoke. After a while, there was more smoke. Somehow, Wakonda got a spark to into the hay at the bottom of the logs. After that, it wasn't long before there was a whole fire blazing up.

In front of the big campfire, Miss Macon gave prizes to campers who were going home. Most were camp letters you could sew on your shirt. Some were pins for swimming. Sally and Ann got candles and floated them out. Ann was going home too. They lived in the same place and were friends from before.

Sally cried. She was sorry to go home. I wasn't sorry. Sally did mean things and Ann helped her. Once, Sally threw all the clothes from my shelves on the floor and walked on them. Another time, she and Ann fixed my bed so I couldn't get my feet down into it.

Why was Sally mean? On the way back to the dorm, Roxanne told me Sally couldn't stay her last week because her father had lost everything. I thought he'd buried it under a tree.

Sunday everyone wore white. No mail came, but parents came to visit. My parents couldn't come because it was too far, Miss Heidigger said. Old campers went home. There was chicken dinner for everyone. Afterwards, we were supposed to take naps, but no one was lying on the beds. Sally had gone, and Miss Heidigger had told me I was going to be alone. No other little girl was coming.

When I went out the back door of the dorm again, I still didn't find my candy, but I found something else. I'd heard big boys talk about the lean-to where they could sleep out in sleeping bags. I found the lean-to. It was open in front, and in back where the log roof slanted down, there was hay. I could smell it. It was dark inside, so I didn't climb in. I ran.

On Monday of my second week at camp, I finished the red and white boondoggle for my father and started another one. Since no letter had come and maybe my mother and father were lost somewhere, the boondoggle was for me. It was white. That was because Miss Betty and I liked white. Miss Betty and I were best friends, and she showed me a magazine with pictures of white dresses. It was a brides' magazine. Afterwards, Roxanne told me Miss Betty wanted to be a bride. Her groom would be the bugle boy.

Tuesday, Miss Betty was sorry I didn't get a letter. It was almost time for lunch, but she stayed back to untangle a mistake I'd made in my boondoggle. "Lil," she told me, "I have a secret."

Would she tell me? When the bugle started blowing, she did. It was—she had picked her dress. She showed it to me in the brides' magazine, and it was the one with the biggest skirt. The skirt went all over the floor in ripples like ripples on the lake.

Miss Betty gave my boondoggle back to me, all fixed. "Lil, do you have a secret?"

I looked at her. Her hair was dark and curled almost the way my mother's was. After a long time, looking down at my boondoggle, I said: "I want my mother, but if she can't come for me, I want you to take me home with you."

It was true. I'd been thinking about it. Roxanne wasn't old enough to be my mother. Miss Heidigger and Miss Macon were too old, and besides, Miss Macon had to take care of Miss Heidigger when she cried. "Miss Betty," I said, "you're the prettiest."

Miss Betty gave me a hug and a kiss too. "Someday Lil," she told me, "I'm going to be the mother of a little girl just like you."

Wednesday, I didn't get my letter, but I did get out of the crib. I was the only one under eight to do it. Miss Macon swam with me, as we went all the way to the raft. When we got there, she boosted me up to climb the ladder. The trouble was—I couldn't get down.

"Jump!" Miss Macon called. She was in the water, holding up her big arms to catch me.

I couldn't jump. I was so cold my teeth were chattering, but I was afraid. If I went too deep, what was underneath? If I couldn't come up would I go to the drowned village?

Miss Macon stayed in the water, reaching up. She was big, she was smiling. She was wearing her blue bathing suit. Maybe she was as cold as I was, but she didn't swim away or get mad. When I did jump, we were both very happy. I even did it again. After that, I wasn't afraid of jumping.

The next morning, Thursday, a letter came, but it wasn't from my mother. It was from my father, and Miss Heidigger read it to me. My mother had been in the hospital, but she was all right. He was coming to get me on Sunday, and the best thing was—she was coming with him. I thought Sunday was a long time, but Miss Heidigger said it was only three days away. I was happy.

On Friday morning it was almost raining, so Roxanne and I walked to riding on the black tar road. When we got there, we were the only ones. Roxanne said the boys who rode Fritz and Humbert had gone home.

Since it was my last time, Herr Schmidt took me out on the trails with Roxanne. When we got back, it was raining a lot. As Herr Schmidt lifted me down he said, "I too am leaving, Scats."

I was surprised. "Are you going to Vienna?"

"Only going."

I wanted to ask why he wasn't going to where the Lipizzaners lived, but he looked so sad I didn't. Water was dripping from the brim of his big, brown hat. "My home is gone, Scats."

From the was he said it, I knew not to ask him where. Instead, I told him good-bye the way he'd taught me.

"Auf Wiedersehen."

"Auf Wiedersehen."

When Roxanne and I ran down the tar road to the crafts shack, I saw the footprints we had made were still there. They were full of water. "Herr Schmidt's going to another camp," she panted.

"Why?" I was trying to keep up.

"There aren't enough campers here to support a riding teacher. They may have to close before the end of August. I heard there isn't one new camper coming Sunday."

At crafts, Miss Betty seemed as sad as Herr Schmidt. We finished my white boondoggle, and to make her happy, I put it around her neck. "I love you."

"Oh Lil—" She smiled, but only a little. Then she gave it back. She was still sad. Didn't she like white any more? Where was her brides' magazine? Was it just the rain? Had she been crying?

At lunch, Miss Heidigger was only there a little while. She didn't even eat her bean soup. She had to go back to the little office by the kitchen where Miss Macon had a typewriter. She had to write letters.

After lunch the sun came out, but I was tired from riding the trails. Miss Macon and Miss Heidigger weren't there to tell me, but I lay on my cot. Down the hall, Roxanne and some big girls were talking, but I didn't hear what they said. Maybe I went to sleep, maybe I didn't. Anyway, the picture was in my mind of the tree where I'd buried my candy and the grey stone. At the same time, I saw the drowned village where lost things were. Herr Schmidt's home in Vienna was there, so was Sally's father's house.

When I got up and went our the back door, nobody noticed.

It wasn't time for swimming yet. Miss Macon hadn't come to take off her little black watch and put on her big blue bathing suit. In the woods, right in front of me, I found my tree. My grey stone was there. I dug with it in the needles. I found my jar of candy!

I picked it up—then I had to drop it. Outside the jar and inside too because the top was loose, mean little black ants were crawling. I felt as if there were ants in my stomach too. There was an ant on my finger. First I squashed him, then I ran.

By mistake, I ran the wrong way, not to the dorm to look for Miss Macon or Miss Heidigger. I was at the lean-to, but not at the open part in front. I was at the back where you couldn't see inside. I heard something. It was fighting, it was growling. It was a cat, dog or person singing. I had to go to the bathroom, but I was too scared to run. One voice was almost like Miss Betty's. Why was she crying? Was the other voice the bugle boy's? Where was his bugle?

The back of the lean-to was logs like the rest of it. There were little cracks between the logs. Through one of the cracks I saw something. Were they fighting? Why were they fighting lying down? My stomach ached a lot, and I had to go to the bathroom a lot. I didn't want to look through the crack any more.

Did they hear me run away? Was that why the cat meowing and the dog growling stopped? Who was laughing?

Before I found the dorm, I got sick. I was so sick some yellow pee came down my leg. Everything I'd had for lunch came up and went down into the pine needles. There weren't any ants, but I thought they were coming. The coughing noise I made throwing up was almost a dog voice.

When I was washing myself in the dorm, Miss Heidigger found me. I was so glad to see her, I cried. She helped me into my bathing suit. I wanted to swim to the raft and jump into deep water, maybe even as far down as the drowned village.

23

"I'm sorry what we had for lunch didn't agree with you," Miss Heidigger said.

"I don't like bean soup."

"I don't, either."

Miss Heidigger looked so sad I didn't tell her about the ants or the meow growling. I didn't want to make her cry. Then Miss Macon came in her blue bathing suit and we went down to the lake together.

Saturday night was my last night at camp. Before campfire, we had to go to supper by the ringing of the bell in the chapel. There was no bugle. The bugle boy had run away. Roxanne said he hadn't been paid, but another big girl said no, he had gone to join the Army. At supper, Miss Betty was still there. Her table was for bigger girls. She looked white and sad.

Maybe Wakonda had been paid, maybe he hadn't, but he was at the campfire. He made fire in the dark again, and the smoke billowed up. When the fire got big and bright, Miss Macon gave out the awards. I got two. I was surprised. One was for being the youngest camper. It was a camp letter to sew on your shirt. The other was a little gold pin. It was for swimming. The pin looked like a wave.

When I floated my good-bye candle out on the lake, I watched it a long time. Then I couldn't see it anymore. Did it go to the drowned village?

Sunday morning I woke up early. I thought maybe they would come for breakfast. Then Miss Heidigger said my parents would come in the afternoon. They had a long way to drive. I kept looking down the road to the stone pillars.

When I was playing with Roxanne, they came. Our green car was in front of the girls' dorm! They were early! They had come Saturday and spent the night with my grandfather who didn't live so far away. Oh, my mother was so pretty and smelled so good! We sat on the porch of the dorm, and I sat in my mother's lap in the rocking chair. I was glad to see my father, I was glad to see my grandfather, but it was my mother I had wanted every night.

Miss Macon came out on the porch and told them about my swimming. Miss Heidigger came out and told them I was "a good little camper." I was so happy— I showed my family everything. We went to the lake and then the riding ring, and coming back, I showed them my tar footprint. I didn't take them to the woods where I'd dropped the sourball jar. Was that near the lean-to? I didn't remember. I didn't want to take them there.

Last of all, we went to the crafts shack. Miss Betty was there. She wanted to pick me up and kiss me good-bye, but I was naughty. I hid behind my mother's back. My mother shook her hand instead. I didn't like Miss Betty's white cat face. She smelled of hay.

I gave the blue and white boondoggle to my mother, and she liked it. I gave the red and white boondoggle to my father, and he liked it. Because I didn't know my grandfather was coming, I didn't have a boondoggle for him. So I gave him mine. That was all right. I didn't like white any more.

When we were leaving the crafts shack, Miss Betty called: "Good-bye, Lil."

I wouldn't answer. Then my mother told me to say good-bye, so I called back: "Only my mother can call me Lil."

At the dorm, Miss Heidigger had packed my suitcase. It was all ready at the top of the porch steps, and my father put it in the car. We weren't staying for chicken dinner, we were going to my grandfather's. After that, even though it was a long way, we were driving home. My father wasn't going to lose his job. He had to go to work in the morning.

When Miss Macon and Miss Heidigger were saying good-bye to us, my father said, "I guess Lillian wants to come back next summer," and my mother nodded.

I wanted to tell them I didn't want to come back, but there wasn't time. We were in the car. I was sitting beside my grandfather looking out the back window. The black road was behind us, we passed the stone posts. We were on our way home.

After we got home, my mother told me she had lost the baby. Talking about him made her cry. I cried too. She took me on her lap and told me how glad she was to have me.

"You won't lose me?"

"Never, Lil," she promised, "never, ever."

That winter, I thought about how I got what I wanted—my mother—but no one else did. Later, my father told me the two old maid school teachers—he meant Miss Macon and Miss Heidigger—had lost the camp. When I did go back the next summer, the new head counselors were Mr. and Mrs. Childs. Their little girl was five, but I was six and didn't have to be the youngest. Mrs. Childs was a good cook. We didn't have to eat beans anymore.

Sally didn't come back to camp. The bugle boy didn't either, and I never saw Miss Betty or Herr Schmidt again. What was the same the next summer and the summers after was the campfire. Wakonda still came and made fire in the dark. The tar road still smelled the same, and the main camp buildings still looked the same, but the lean-to fell down one winter. After a while, trees grew up where the hay had been. I didn't like to go there, but later, I forgot why.

Those summers waned slowly. I never swam as far as the drowned village, but each year my candle floated toward it—and got lost. Losses of more than wax and fire lay in the distance, but in the sheltering darkness, I couldn't see them.

The Neighbors

We moved there the spring I was eight. It was a modest, maple-lined suburban street of houses build a decade earlier in the Twenties—before The Crash.

While the last of the scratched and battered antiques which were the treasured and polished remnants of my parents' pre-1929 hopes were still being unloaded, I wandered down the short driveway where grass was poking up amidst sparse gravel. Then I went across the street to meet the neighbors.

Directly opposite our house, in a front yard where there were lots of dandelions, I saw a girl who was about my size. She was standing on the stoop with her hand on the door handle as if about to go in.

I went up the walk. "Do you want to play?"

"I can't. I have to watch the baby—he's asleep."

"Oh." I had no such responsibilities; I was an only child. My parents' other baby had died before I was born.

"Do you want to come inside?" she demanded, opening the door. "I'm Betty Rodericks."

I followed her into the dimness of her front hall, which had wallpaper with grey and brown flowers. Her house smelled faintly of diapers, and perhaps of the kind of talcum powder that came in the can with red roses on it.

Already, I saw she was prettier than I was. Her hair was blonde, and she had pink skin to go with it. My hair was a muddy brown, and my skin was sallow. I knew I would have to tell her my name, but I waited until after we had checked the baby, who was sleeping peacefully in a battered wicker perambulator on the screen porch in back.

Finally, when we had gone upstairs to the room she shared with her younger sister, I drew a deep breath. "I'm Adelaide—Adelaide Miller." I would have given anything to have been Susan, Jane or, yes, Betty. Adelaide was not the sort of short, stylish name that friends, if you had them, called across the school yard. It was an old-fashioned name that was not easily shortened. It had belonged to my grandmother.

Adelaide, in the place where we had lived since kindergarten in a house that hardly even had a yard, was the girl who had been left back in first grade because she was slow in learning to read the teacher's flash cards. She was the girl who was inevitably the last in line, and the one, when the time came to choose, who was without a partner.

"What grade are you in?" I demanded.

"Second."

"I'm in third," I told her quickly.

"Do you race?"

"Race?"

"You know, the hundred yard dash, the fifty yard dash. Here they have races down in the park on Memorial Day and on Fourth of July too. Last year, I won the first and second grade races for girls both times."

I had never seen trophies before, but she showed me hers, which were neatly arranged on the lace cover of the bureau she and her sister used. Each was a shiny figure on a white pedestal reaching for the stars.

The baby began to cry, and then, my mother called me. On the way out, I met Betty's mother, who had come home from taking Betty's sister to the doctor. The sister, whose name was Lorna, had a rash.

At my house, my mother had set out a sandwich wrapped in wax paper for me in the breakfast nook in the kitchen. She was trying to persuade the painters, who had arrived soon after the moving man, to mix some pink paint for the walls of my room instead of using the shiny tan they had used for everything else.

The house was only rented, so she didn't have much say, but she finally got them to mix in something that made my room not really pink, but a pale brick color. Unlike my mother and father, I barely remembered the little white house with wallpaper in every room which we had owned in our home town way upstate. That was the house—I had heard them say— on which the mortgage had been foreclosed. That had happened because the company my father was working for closed its doors.

When my father came up the walk from the 6:30 train that night—it had taken him three years to find a job, and he usually stayed at the office late—the movers were still struggling. Having the painters there at the same time hadn't helped, and the two men were trying to guide my mother's father's grand piano between the evergreens that flanked the front walk. My father took off his coat and tie and helped them, and they finally maneuvered it into the corner of the narrow living room, where the bowed part of the instrument stuck out awkwardly in front of the door to the screen porch.

Still, the piano was beside a window. When we raised the sash after dinner, there was a nice breeze from the back yard. My father, who had a gentle, mellow, baritone voice, took his songs out of the piano seat and played for a while. Making my way among the packing cases, I sat down on the bench beside him. I forgot that my name was Adelaide. I was happy.

The next morning—it was spring vacation and we didn't have school until Monday— Betty and I went around the neighborhood gathering people for races which would take place in my driveway since at her house we might wake the baby.

Riding up and down the block on our bikes, we gathered three others. Clyde, who lived next door to Betty, was in third but was smaller then either of us. He had a very long, straight nose and a small mouth and looked like a ferret. He was very quiet, and I suspected he did not like his name any better than I did mine. Deirdre, a big girl—she was in fifth—joined us that day but moved away soon afterwards. The last was Lorna, Betty's sister, who went to kindergarten.

My mother was in the back yard, beating the dust out of the

oriental rugs and the down-stuffed sofa cushions with a long rattan paddle. For a while, after she was finished, she let us take down her clotheslines and use them as markers.

Of course, Betty won nearly everything. At the end, she even beat Deirdre, who had red hair and got overheated easily. I didn't have a chance from the beginning, but what made it worse was that, in the middle of everything, I slid on a grass tuft and fell flat, breaking off half of one of my upper front teeth. Betty grabbed up the useless piece from the gravel, and when I ran inside crying, they all followed, tracking across the kitchen floor my mother was mopping.

Afterwards, that tooth added considerably to my parents' debts—first for the caps which were never quite the right color and sometimes fell off, and finally, for the abscess in the jaw. Even then though, while my mother was sponging the knee I had bloodied with boric acid on a piece of cotton, I knew there was justice in it.

For, in the very race in which I had fallen, I had, without anyone's noticing, inched forward to get a head start, hoping— just once—to win. Then, after the others had gone home and my mother had called my father at work to see if he could get someone to recommend a dentist, I compounded what I had done with a lie.

"Was there anything that made you fall?" my mother wanted to know.

"No," I told her, "nothing."

Several years later, when I had to go to the hospital to have a place in the jaw above the dead tooth cut out, I wasn't surprised. The entire procedure—choking on the anesthetic, waking up alone in the dark room and vomiting blood on the floor, going home dizzy in the morning with my lip swollen like Pinnocchio's nose so my father wouldn't be charged for a second day—was inevitable. It was the natural result of desperately sneaking the toe of one of the ugly brown oxfords my mother had chosen for me against her limp, white line.

After that I still tried to win sometimes—mainly by fair means—but my hopes were not extravagant. I was getting used to "<u>Ad</u>-a-lade," which was the way the teachers said my name when I didn't answer their questions quickly or when I was immersed in reading (which I was beginning to like) and didn't hear them. I knew Adelaide wasn't going to win any trophies.

By the time summer vacation came, Betty and I were best friends, and she had already won the Memorial Day races again. We played almost daily in the lots—the overgrown, empty place between Betty's house and the next one down the mild slope of the street. No house had been built there because if you went way back—the path twisted between burrs and poison ivy— you came to the landlocked one-story former farmhouse where Elaine lived.

Elaine didn't have parents like the rest of us. Instead she lived with her grandmother, who was bent and wrinkled and had trouble getting between the oilcloth-covered table and the black iron stove in her stone-floored kitchen. She was even older than Betty's grandmother, who had come to live recently and, so my mother said, made things hard for Mrs. Rodericks because there were only three bedrooms and now all the children had to be crowded into the same one.

After the lots—where we arranged houses for our dolls hidden behind bushes and   hillocks—we were allowed to come out again after supper. We played Red Rover or—the one I liked best—Giant Steps, until it got dark. Those games were no good with only two, so we would go and get Clyde, who listened to the radio a lot and wrote in to the programs for things like magic rings and invisible ink. The night Clyde won Giant Steps three times running—he had long spidery legs which came in handy with scissor steps—he was wearing a Tom Mix ring with a red stone, and I got the idea he believed it helped him.

Even three wasn't much for those games, and Betty's sister

31

Lorna always had to go in early. Often too, if we ran through the lots calling for Elaine, we found there was no one home.

So, since there were no other children on our street, we cut through my backyard to get the two boys who lived side by side on the next block. Bobo—the bully—was heavyset, with hair that grew straight up. Jamie—his victim—had a head like an upended peanut where only a little hair grew. Not only was Jamie's father dead—an odd thing in itself—his mother, so my mother said, hadn't been very well when she was having him. That was why his arms were like matchsticks and his skin was grey and transparent.

Anyway, Jamie was skinny enough to make you turn around in the street and stare, and Bobo had no difficulty in beating him up as often as he wanted. Jamie stayed inside his room a lot of the time. He had a desk that he always kept perfectly neat. There wasn't a speck of dust, and every pencil was in place. Once, when Bobo wasn't calling up from the bushes under the window to taunt him to come out and fight, he showed it to me. He even had a globe map of the earth that lighted up from inside.

Then in August when it had been hot for a long time, Betty couldn't play. She had poison ivy. Elaine wasn't home, and Deirdre had moved, so I was thrown back on the three boys— mainly Clyde because Bobo and Jamie were absorbed in their perpetual battles. Clyde liked a game where he drew a circle in a dusty spot in his back yard and we each threw bubble gum war cards into it one by one, taking turns calling heads or tails, winner take both.

I won at that about as much as Clyde did, but there wasn't a lot of satisfaction in it, so I took to spending afternoons with my grandfather, who had come down from upstate where we used to live for a visit. He couldn't see well—he sometimes bumped into a door he thought was open which someone had left shut—but he could recite poetry by the hour.

I could be doing something else—arranging my dolls on the

angular patterns of our frayed rugs—while he gave me "the Charge of the Light Brigade," "Barbara Fritchie," or "The Children's Hour."

Then, after he went back to the place my parents still called home, Betty was allowed out again, but we always had to play at my house. Her grandmother had gone to the hospital and died, and her brother had caught Lorna's rash. Her mother had printed a note on their screen door that read: "BABY SLEEP-ING. PLEASE DON'T RING."

Sometimes, when even Betty was tired of racing because she always won, we would pick out names that would be ours when we grew up. She wavered between Lady Esther, which was what it said on her mother's face powder box, and La Verne, which she felt obligated to pick because it had been her grandmother's. I always took the same one. It was Star.

"Movie star?" Betty asked once.

"No—just Star."

Just a few days before school started, Betty's father, who had had his job a long time and went to the city in the morning on the late train instead of the early one my father took, drove the whole family to the shore for a vacation. It was the week of my birthday, but there was no one to come to a party, so my mother invited a friend of hers who was also from upstate to drive over from another town and bring her little girl for lunch.

Our summer drinks were usually made from the lemon or raspberry syrup that my mother cooked and then put in the refrigerator in jars. That day, besides my cake, we had ginger ale. I had a whole, green bottle to myself, and so did Louise, which was the girl's name.

Louise talked a lot about bucks, which she had to explain to me meant dollars. "My father has a lot of them," she told me, "does yours?"

"No. I don't think so."

Then seeing it wasn't always so good to tell the truth, I got her to come out on the screen porch with her ginger ale. "Let's race," I said, "and see who can finish the bottle first."

She did it right away, but I held back. I knew there wouldn't be any more ginger ale coming, and I had quite a lot left. I drank it slowly, after hers was empty, and didn't offer her a sip.

My mother was busy inside the house most of the time. She cleaned a lot. Before Betty came back, because there was no one else, I even went around and talked to grownups like Jo Ellen, who lived next door.

She asked me to call her that, and my mother said it was all right— even though she was really Mrs. Hailley. Her baby—a girl that was named after her—was only a year old. In her living room, she had a picture of herself in her wedding gown that still looked something like her, even though her hair wasn't curled the same.

Jo Ellen was making mother-daughter dresses for herself and the baby. While she sewed, she told me about a course which she had taken once in Texas, where she had almost finished college. In the course, she had to learn all of *The Bible*.

"*All* of it?" I couldn't help asking, looking up from the cross stitch dresser scarf for my mother which she was helping me make.

"All of it," she said, biting off her thread and looking me straight in the eye, "—every verse."

Afterwards, I asked my mother about it. She said Jo Ellen—whose husband shouted at her sometimes (we could hear their voices even when their screen porch doors were shut)—might not have remembered exactly. Maybe what she had memorized was not the words but the stories about David and Jonathan and Saul on the Road to Damascus and people like that.

Later, when I was playing after supper on the front walk with the red ball I'd named Ballo, bouncing it a certain number of times in each square on concrete because that set things right, I saw I wasn't the only one who wanted to win enough to lie about it. Even grown-ups did it.

It was Labor Day. My father, who always went to work Saturdays, had been home two days straight. He had trimmed the twin evergreens at the end of the walk to look like upside down ice cream cones. The shadow between them was particularly dark. I bounced Ballo in a circle there and then three times on each of the brick steps of the stoop for good luck. Instead of waiting for my mother to call me, I went in early.

I had decided to start a second dresser scarf which would be almost as nice as my mother's. If I could finish it by Christmas, I would give it to Jo Ellen.

The next winter, Mrs. Rodericks had a birthday party at the end of January for Betty. I was invited, and so were girls from her class who didn't even live near us. There were things I had never had in the dining room with the ice cream and cake—pink and blue crepe paper snappers that contained party hats and prizes, and matching crepe paper baskets full of candy. The best part for me, though, was the scene Betty's mother had made in the living room.

Mrs. Rodericks, whose stomach was very big—my mother had explained to me that she was going to have another baby—had piled up a lot of white cotton on the mantelpiece to look like snow. On it, all around a nice little round mirror that looked like an ice skating rink, were pipe stem figures of children which she herself had dressed in tiny suits and skirts and hats. Of course, we could not touch the arrangement, but I liked looking at it, particularly when she turned on a music box hidden under one of the hills of cotton and it played "The Skaters' Waltz."

After she had wound the music box more than once, Mrs. Rodericks sat down in a soft chair beside a picture of herself. It wasn't like Jo Ellen's picture. It was brown-toned instead of black and white, and it had been taken even before she was a bride. She had had beautiful long curls that she didn't have any more at all. In fact her hair, which was pinned up and wispy, was getting almost as grey as her mother's had been.

Mrs. Rodericks saw me looking at her picture. Maybe she even saw what I was thinking about. "I wanted to be an artist then," she started to tell me, but then the baby spit up his chocolate ice cream all over the front of the pretty little blue suit she had made for him. After that, the phone rang, and I never heard any more about it.

When the war came, some things changed. My father, who now only worked half a day on Saturdays, was the air raid block captain. My mother, who now had a woman who came to wash clothes and clean once a week, spent a long time sewing blackout curtains for the cellar windows.

The lots were no longer our playground. They had been divided up into plots for Victory Gardens, and every neighbor had one. My father's plot was full of stones. He grew a lot of tomatoes anyway, but his carrots were crooked. The stones changed them. By the end of the summer, his hands peeled all over from working in the soil.

He tried what the doctor told him, but it didn't help. The cleaning woman, a Ukranian, told him to try warm milk. After dinner, my mother washed the dishes, and it took a long time because she washed them and rinsed them and then dried the silver and china with a special towel. So he would come out and sit with me on the screen porch where I read the books I had begun to take out of the library in piles. He had the milk in a white enamel pitcher on a towel on his lap. He would hold his hands in. First one, then the other.

At last, my father had a vacation. A whole week. We went home—back upstate to the place we had all been born—and visited my grandfather. We even had a new car to drive in, a grey Chevrolet. Somehow I remembered the road when we got near there. The smell was familiar. In the back seat, squashed in with the luggage and the little green trunk that held my dolls' clothes, I sang to myself: "We're on the road home. We're on the road *home*."

Up there, we drove around and saw my parents' friends and places I wasn't sure I remembered but almost did because I had heard so much about them. There was the big yellow brick house with the iron fences where my mother had lived with her mother and father long before they lost all their money in The Crash and died. There was the church where my parents had gotten married, which had a little window with the Christ Child and a white lamb. There was the cemetery where most of the older people were—my father's father was the last one left.

My grandfather had even had his stone set there by my grandmother's. It had his name and birth date, but the death date was blank—a shiny rectangle of raised, grey stone.

Behind the big stones, in the depression in the center of the plot was a little, flat, shoe box sized stone that only said "BABY" and the date. It was our baby, my mother reminded me. There was something wrong with his head. Then, going around to the other side of the little stone, she hid her face from us and cried.

On the way back to where we lived, we stopped at a cavern where they had colored lights on the stalactites and the stalagmites. We even took a boat ride on an underground river, so I had something to tell Betty, who always told me what she had done at the shore. I even had colored post cards of the cavern, and I mounted them in a black leather album my grandfather had given me.

Telling Betty wasn't quite so important, though, because I had a new friend, Mary Lou, who was in my own class. It was all right for me to go to Mary Lou's house after school even though she lived four blocks away—as long as I called my mother when I got there. On afternoons when I knew Betty would have to stay in to watch her baby sister, I often went to Mary Lou's where we were working on our paper dolls.

Mary Lou was very good at drawing—the best in our class, the teacher said. She helped me with my paper doll, which was wearing a black bathing suit. Then, after we had each mounted our doll on heavy cardboard and cut it out, we began to make wardrobes copied from her mother's magazines.

The year after our vacation, my grandfather died. It was the middle of the winter, so we all went up on the train instead of driving, sitting in a compartment with green plush seats and khaki colored curtains you could pull across the windows.

My father had to stand in my grandfather's front parlor where my grandfather was in his coffin—except it didn't look like him at all. A lot of people came and shook my father's hand.

When it was time to go, the house was being sold—we might not ever come home again—I walked through every room and looked at the way things were. Then, when I was back in my own bed in the place we lived, I would go through every room in my mind before I went to sleep—so I wouldn't forget.

On the little curio shelf in the corner of my room, I put the miniature book my grandfather had given me. It was the size for a doll, and it had its own metal box. It was about two little girls who gave a fair to raise money for Civil War soldiers.

Then, because my grandfather had left my father some money, we bought our own house. It was only about six blocks from our rented house, but it was bigger, and we could paint the walls whatever color we wanted and put paper in the bedrooms. I had paper with pink and white roses tied with blue ribbons, and there was a glass porch adjoining where I had a shelf that went all the way to the ceiling for my books.

It was my first year in Junior High, and Betty was still in grade school. I had invited her to my birthday party, but she was going on vacation. Clyde and Bobo and Jamie were in

Junior High with me, but it was a big school. I only saw them once in a while in the halls.

Mary Lou was my best friend, and she knew other girls we did things with. She even had a party where boys came and danced, and she helped me make one of the gathered, flowered skirts we were all supposed to wear.

We lived in that house all the time I was in high school, and then I went away to college. In the middle of the first year I was there, I got the phone call from my mother about my father.

When I got home after the ten hour train ride, she told me he had shot himself in the extra bedroom upstairs. He had never gotten over what had happened to him in The Depression, she said, and he hadn't been promoted to the big job he wanted at work. When I went upstairs and looked in that room, I saw the blood all over the yellow wallpaper.

My mother re-papered the room. Then she sold the house and the grand piano and rented an apartment where she could fit most of the other antiques. I got a scholarship so I could finish college. Her apartment was on the other side of town. It was a ways from where Mary Lou or anyone else I knew lived, but I had learned to drive and my mother still had the Chevrolet, so I still saw them sometimes.

After I graduated though, my mother moved again. She didn't go home upstate. She said she didn't know people there anymore. She said she had always wanted to live at the shore— even though she was worried that the salt air might damage the antiques. She had heard of jobs there. I saw that there were things she had wanted besides the dead baby.

The last weekend I went out to see her before she left for the waves and sand, I met Betty at the station Monday morning where we were both waiting for trains.

She was still blonde and prettier than I was, but her high heeled, open toed pumps suggested that she didn't race any more. She was wearing a soft, pleated, navy blue dress with a lace collar. It was a little too frilly to be stylish, but I suspected that her mother had spent a long time making it.

She had read about my father in the newspapers, and she said she was sorry. I thanked her. Both her parents were fine, and so were the other children. Even the babies were in high school. Clyde and the other neighbors still lived there, and Jamie's mother had married again and Jamie went hunting with his new father. Only Elaine was gone, no one knew where. Elaine's grandmother's house had been torn down, and the land around it combined with the lots to make a park.

I didn't tell her my mother was moving and I wouldn't be coming back. I just said that I'd rented a room in the city near the bookstore where I was working. She was working too, as a secretary, and, just as the rails began to hum and we heard the whistle at the bend, she told me she was engaged to Clyde. She showed me her ring, which I should have noticed but hadn't, and a picture of him which I wouldn't have recognized. Clyde had grown up big and broad shouldered, and he hardly looked at all like a ferret any more.

The house I had lived in was up for sale, Betty told me as the cars of her train rattled in front of us and the brakes squealed. Her parents and Clyde's were thinking of helping them with the down payment. "It's nice to be where you know the neighbors," she said as she climbed aboard.

"Of course," I said, pretending I could picture it. For a moment, I imagined Betty might have a daughter who would win all the races in my driveway. They would probably paper my room for her.

"Good-bye Adelaide," she called down to me.

The name didn't make me wince. It was what I had left, and I was thinking of making something of it. I waved and stepped back. Her train slid past me—we were going in different directions. I still had a few minutes to wait for my train, which was the one my father had always ridden.

In the Dust

I've dared myself. I'm going to write the truth no matter what. That truth is: I've always been afraid of big boys. Even now that I'm in fifth grade, I'm not over it. I've had them chase me home in winter with iceballs. I've had them drive me inside my house in summer with gravel from my own driveway. Big boys throw hard. They hit what they want to hit, and when they hit, it hurts.

Today though, I, Imogene Lois Mattherson—ten, going on eleven—got brave. I went where some of those same boys were, and I didn't run away—at least not until the dust had settled and the blood had bled.

It happened because of the Long Cut. The Long Cut is the long way of walking home I've made up since school started. Last summer, when kids play I play with were on vacation, I played board games by myself because I don't have brothers or sisters. This fall, I invented the Long Cut, which is like those games, but real.

In Parcheesi and other games I have that used to be my father's, you try to reach HOME. The Long Cut is like that, but my trick is: you don't go by the four and a half blocks of sidewalk squares. Instead, you skip through back yards, across open spaces, along hedges and up driveways of people even my mother doesn't know.

Our town is built on the side of a hill of which the other side is still woods. The sidewalks to my house slope down a little or stay flat, but a lot of kids take them. The Long Cut is uphill and around, but sometimes I get all the way home without meeting anyone at all.

Most days, I don't take the Long Cut home at lunch, only after school. My mother always has lunch ready, and I'm not supposed to be late. If I'm late, it could make her late getting back to her new job at the bank.

Today at noon though, I heard something that sounded like

41

an ambulance down the hill. I hate the way those sirens wail, so I turned up and crossed Ridgewood Road—a wide street even if there aren't many cars on it—to the driveway of the big grey stucco house where the Long Cut begins.

Then, as I climbed the drive, two big boys came up behind me from nowhere. I was scared, but they streaked past me as if I wasn't there. One was George McIntyre from the sixth. The other was Bill Ferguson, a redhead and the biggest boy in my class. George was chasing Bill, and behind them came some other sixth grade boys, running fast. As he passed me, the last one panted: "Fight."

When I got to the hedge at the top of the drive, I saw it. In the backyard between piles of yellow and brown leaves, George and Bill were lying in the dust, hitting each other.

I was afraid to go forward, but I didn't want to give up the game and go back. So I kept behind the hedge and waited, hoping for the fight to be over. Instead, it went on.

The fight was all fists and shouts. Maybe there had been a quarrel to start it, but it was really a game to win. The aim was for one to knock the other in the dust and keep him there. When George got to his knees, Bill pulled him down. When Bill rolled away suddenly and stood up, George tackled and toppled him back. Sometimes, when a breeze raised the leaves and dust, you could hardly see who was winning. They were buried together.

It was getting late, but I couldn't get up my courage to run by them. In Parcheesi, when an enemy gets two men on a square ahead of you, you can't pass. Finally, I cheated a little, edging out beyond the hedge to behind the trunk of a big apple tree. Then, as quickly as it had begun, the fight was over. The boys ran—some down the driveway, some up the hill. Only one was left. It was Bill. He was still lying in the leaves, and I could hear him crying.

I was sure then I wouldn't have trouble getting across the yard to the place where the Long Cut goes by the falling down fences of two old tennis courts. Still, remembering the ice balls, I picked up a yellow apple from the ground—just in case.

Crossing the yard, even though I tried to be quiet, was noisy because of the leaves. Even so, I would have made it past the place where Bill was lying with his arms over his head, except—I sneezed.

It was dust. I couldn't help it. I sneezed again. Naturally, Bill heard me. He sat up.

I could have, should have dashed past him, but the way he looked stopped me. His red hair was darkened by dust, his milky face was brightened by blood. There were leaves all over his clothes, and one eye was swollen shut. The worst part was his mouth. Blood from his nose, which was still bleeding, was crusted on his lips. Maybe he'd swallowed some too, because when he said: "What do you want?" in a quavery voice, I saw blood slavering around his tongue.

"Nothing," I told him, trying to sidle by. I should have moved faster, but I had to stare. Those places where he'd been hit must hurt. I remembered the thud of the ice ball in the small of my back. I was beginning to get a stomach ache.

Slowly, he wiped his nose with the back of his hand. Then he wiped the hand on some leaves and stood up. Then, kicking at some of the leaves so the dust rose again, he said: "you want to be next?"

What did he mean? Did he mean to fight? Did he mean to knock me down in the dust? My heart was pounding, my fingers were digging through the skin of the apple into its inside softness.

Stepping closer, he gave me a little push—not hard enough to knock me over. "Where'd you get that apple?" he demanded in a mean way.

I nodded toward the big tree.

"You took it—"

"It was lying on the *ground*—"

That made him angry. "You stole it—so *eat* it." Snatching

43

it from me, he forced my mouth wide.

It was an old, dusty apple, not a good apple. Maybe it had a worm in it. I bit, retched, choked. Finally, he released me. I only sobbed once, maybe twice, but I couldn't stop the tears from coming out of my eyes.

He looked at me as if I was less than dust. He still had what was left of the apple in his hand. Then, taking it in his bloody fingers, he threw it high and hard the way boys do—and smashed it into the trunk of its own tree. There was nothing left then but seeds in apple ooze sliding down the bark.

Why didn't I run? I was still standing like a dumb statue when he said: "Your father died."

"So what." Everybody in the fifth knew my father died of cancer in May before school ended. He was taken to the hospital in an ambulance a few weeks before, but it was too late. He never got home again.

"You're stupid. Im-*o*-gene."

"*You're* stupid. You lost the fight."

"He's bigger—"

I could see he was about to run. I didn't want him to. I wanted—

"My mother died. She died having me." He said it flat out. Then, reaching down and gathering up as many leaves as he could, he threw them all over me. "Fuck you. Fuck *you*."

Maybe he stayed there a minute, maybe he didn't. I ran and I didn't stop running until I was way past the tennis courts and almost home. By that time, most of the leaves had blown off me, but I had to stop to wipe blood from around my mouth. Some of it was from his hands, I guess, but some of it was mine. The apple had stretched one corner of my mouth into a cut. Pretty soon, though, it stopped bleeding.

My mother wasn't angry, just worried. I told her I'd fallen in some leaves. The soup she'd set out for me was cold. I didn't have a stomach ache, but I wasn't hungry. I told my mother I didn't want my sandwich because someone had given me an apple to eat on the way home.

I got back to school on time, but Bill didn't. He came in late with a note from his mother saying he wasn't feeling well. His eye was swollen shut. By that time, I'd found out he had a new mother, a stepmother.

When school let out, it was raining. My mother can't pick me up at school any more now that she's working. I decided to go home by the sidewalks and count the squares. I did that a long time ago, but I didn't write it down. It was a big number, and I forgot.

Today, when I'd only counted to 68, a car stopped beside me. Bill was sitting in the front seat, and a pretty blonde woman was driving. She was his stepmother, and she offered me a ride.

By that time it was pouring, so without even stopping to put a stone on the 68th square so I'd remember it, I got in. I sat in the back seat, and Bill didn't turn around once the whole time I was in the car. Mrs. Ferguson was nice, though. She asked how my mother was doing, and I told her.

When I started this, I promised I'd write the truth. Now I'm almost finished. I have the radio on in the kitchen and the TV on here, and I'm working on my arithmetic. Soon, I'll start the casserole Mom left so dinner will be ready when she gets here. What I'm *really* doing, though, is beginning another game of Parcheesi.

My father's Parcheesi board has 96 squares. That's not counting HOME. The squares are square, but HOME is the circle where all the squares meet. In the new game I'm making up to be played out of doors like the Long Cut, HOME won't be my house—it will be a circle somewhere. It may be a circle of stones nobody but me can find. It may be a circle of chalk on a sidewalk block nobody but me can understand. It may be nothing more than a circle in the dust that will disappear when the wind comes, rising with the leaves.

45

Wally and the Waltz

He was 21, but I was only 11. We began—and very nearly ended—as polite strangers.

It was 1940, the first winter of World War II, and my parents were doing what they could. They and other families we knew were inviting airmen from Australia and New Zealand out for weekends in the country.

The boys, as my father called them (he was a veteran of World War I, a Navy man), usually came for just one weekend arranged by the Anzac Club in New York. They were on their way to Britain, they were passing through.

Sometimes though, pilots, gunners, bombardiers visited several times. Perhaps they were waiting for a troop convoy—I don't remember. The Aussies, who came in twos—or threes if somebody's house was big enough—were apt to return to families where the daughters were 16, 18, or 20. At our house, it was only my mother, my father and I.

On the next block, there were two older girls, both beautiful. In late March, on Easter weekend, Jean and Edna's family took in two New Zealand fliers for the first time. Then in April, when my father was telling my mother and me about the Germans in Denmark and Norway, the fliers came again and took the girls to a good-bye evening in New York. Later, I saw the dark-shadowed flash picture. It showed Jean and Edna with the Aussies at a little table in a big nightclub. Both couples were holding hands.

In May, when my father was showing us newspaper maps shaded so you could tell where the Germans were in the Netherlands, Belgium and France, something else happened. My 21-year old cousin, who lived in the next town, got engaged to a 25-year old pilot from Sydney.

Actually, nothing ever came of it, and I never found out why. When you're 11, they don't tell you everything. My mother, a good housekeeper above all, wasn't clever about

46

explaining matters of importance. My father, of course, was working late almost every night at his office in New York. When he did get home, he talked about Winston Churchill.

The first Aussie who came more than once to our house arrived the night before Memorial Day with two others. Those two gravitated very soon to Jean and Edna, but Wally didn't. He was pale and silent; they were ruddy and noisy. Wally attended the American Legion parade downtown in the village with my mother and me.

My father was in the parade, and when we all got home, Wally and my father sat out on the sun porch and talked about Dunkirk while my mother fixed the picnic supper that we ate in the yard early, before the mosquitoes got too bad. My father, who had served on a destroyer in the Aegean and the Black Seas in the First War, described ships crossing the English Channel to rescue thousands and thousands from French beaches while Wally listened.

After Memorial Day, during the battle of France, Wally came back by himself. I didn't know what he thought of me, but I could see he liked my father. His mother was a widow, he told us, and he was the only son. Maybe that was why my mother didn't bother him. My mother wasn't unfriendly, but she made people uncomfortable. For one thing, she was a stickler for manners. If an Aussie helped himself to butter with his own knife instead of with the silver butter server, she would snatch up the whole dish, server and all, and bring in fresh butter from the refrigerator.

Wally didn't do that, but my mother had other quirks. If a guest sat down in one of the straight chairs in the living room, or even in a Boston rocker, she would say she wanted him to have a more comfortable place on the couch, and so, just when the person had started talking, he had to get up and move.

Maybe my mother made Wally move once, maybe she didn't. Anyway, pretty soon Wally always sat on the couch when my father was home. When my father was at the office, Wally sat in his big armchair. The chair had a red brick colored cover, and it made Wally, who had white blond hair and was slightly built, look smaller than he was.

One Sunday night after supper—it was the middle of June by then and the swastika was flying from the Eiffel Tower—my father surprised Wally by playing "Waltzing Matilda" on the piano. He had bought the sheet music on purpose. Wally didn't sing along with us, but he tapped his foot. Wally liked waltzes, it turned out, but the Australian anthem wasn't one of his favorites.

Later, when it was time for me to go to bed, my father told Wally about 1915 and the Campaign of Gallipoli. Australians and New Zealanders, I heard him say, attacked the Turks on Asian beaches in the Dardanelles. My father showed Wally a book about it. More than eight thousand Anzacs landed, it said, but there were more than seven thousand casualties.

It wasn't until another visit—I remember coming home from school on a Friday afternoon and finding him in the living room—that Wally began to enjoy the record player. Now my mother, who spent most of her time cooking and cleaning, was the sort of person who was always telling me—just when I'd gotten comfortable with a book—that I ought to go outside and "get fresh air" and "breathe deep breaths."

Whether she told Wally that or not, I don't know, but it was she, surprisingly, who suggested that it was all right anytime for Wally to use the new record player, which had been my father's present from his wealthy brother at Christmas. So, instead of leafing through the newspaper and then letting it fall to the floor or taking one of the books from my father's shelves, and then, very soon, putting it back, Wally began to play records—some of which were so old that my father had bought them in college. It was hot by that time, so Wally sat in the living room with the blinds half drawn, working his way from my father's Cornell songs and Caruso records to the popular selections friends had given me at my tenth birthday party.

Finally, at the end of the month when my father was talking about Petain and Laval and Vichy, Wally spotted my mother's old album of Strauss waltzes on a high shelf in the coat closet. It was the middle of the week—not a weekend—and I was finally out of school. Wally had to be back in New York on Saturday morning—it was his last time. Of course he couldn't say when he'd be leaving, but we knew that he wouldn't be with us for the Fourth of July.

The Strauss album had four ten-inch records, and Wally had two days left. On Thursday, I got so I could distinguish between "Tales from the Vienna Woods," "Vienna Dreams," and "Artists' Life." By lunch time on Friday, I had learned the words—not only to "The Blue Danube" but to all the others. I bought Wally a cheese sandwich and a Coke and set it on the radiator beside my father's chair, but I didn't sit down with him, I went back to my room. My mother—she was always doing something like that—was in the attic "going through things."

In my room though, I couldn't get interested in things I usually did. Truthfully, I was thinking about having my long braids cut—but I wasn't sure about it. I guess I was beginning to worry about the big Junior High where I would have to go in the fall. Other girls, I was beginning to realize, had several close girl friends—even a boyfriend. I had neither. Besides that, I was totally flat chested. There were others, already, who were wearing bras.

"Dreams, dreams, Vienna dreams,
"Night time is endless and love supreme...."

I had nothing else to do, so I went downstairs. Of course, Wally was still sitting in my father's big chair. He had drunk the Coke, but he had only eaten the center of the sandwich, leaving the crusts. He looked at me, then he stood up.

It wasn't time to flip the record, we were in the middle of the "Vienna Woods." I stood there. Wally paced across the room. As always, he was military in manner, self-contained.

49

"Miss," he requested in the most formal way imaginable, "would you like to dance?"

Now I had attended dancing class in the school gymnasium for the two previous winters, but no one had ever specifically asked me to dance. At the class, the girls filed in from the left side of the gym and the boys from the right. You had to take the person you were matched with, and then, when it came time to change partners, exchange with the nearest couple.

Somehow though, when Wally asked me, I knew what to do. As if I'd done it a million times before, I said, "I'd be delighted."

We could have been preparing to stroll the Schönbrunn or to mount a coach to Mayerling or some other place I'd never heard of. In any case, I was ready. We repaired to the sun porch and there, positioning ourselves between wicker chairs and tippy little glass-topped tables, we joined hands.

Slowly at first, and then more quickly, we began to twirl. The Wally I'd known on weekends was replaced by another Wally. The new Wally was still formal, still sad—but he was a much better dancer than any of the boys in my class.

At the same time   I don't think I'd ever noticed this about a man except my father before—Wally had his own smell. Perhaps it was shaving lotion, perhaps it was the wool of his uniform. In any case, it reminded me of wet wood.

Wally flipped to "Artists' Life." We had "Voices of Spring" and "The Emperor Waltz." He kept on flipping the records until he was pale no longer—and I was breathless. We stopped abruptly in the middle of the rattan rug, facing each other.

Without introduction, he told me: "I'm afraid."

The record needle was scratching in the groove, but we stood there. He towered over me by a head or more. Quickly, as if I had known all along what he would say, I answered: "I am, too."

Of course, I was thinking about seventh grade, and he was thinking about—more than I could fathom. Still, there was a certain understanding.

I forgot what happened next. No, he didn't kiss me. Soon after that, my father came home from the office early for once, and my mother called us for dinner. She wasn't a conversationalist, but she was a good cook—in a bland, wholesome way. It was roast chicken, and her best homemade chocolate cake. My mother didn't drink, but my father said it was a special occasion, so he and Wally shared some wine.

Later, when I went up to bed, Wally and my father were still talking. As I mounted the stairs, I could hear my father quoting Churchill. "...We shall fight on the beaches, we shall fight on the landing grounds, we shall fight in the fields and in the streets, we shall fight in the hills; we shall never surrender...."

I don't remember saying good-bye to Wally, but I must have. I suppose he and my father took the same train to New York. My father still worked half a day on Saturdays then.

All that summer, the news was bad. My father didn't have to tell us, we could see from the way his face looked when he came home with the paper folded under his arm. Eventually, we had a letter from London, and then, a post card of Dover Beach.

After that, nothing.

Fall came, I started Junior High. It wasn't as bad as I had thought. I made friends with a girl who had just moved to town. She played the violin. She could even scratch out "The Blue Danube."

The Battle of Britain began. I thought about Wally, but no one mentioned him.

It wasn't until after Halloween that my mother had a letter from his mother in Melbourne. Wally's plane had been shot down over the English Channel on the night of a major air victory—September 15. There were no survivors.

That day, my mother was washing curtains, but she didn't finish. Instead, she sat down on the couch and cried.

Afterwards, even though I knew he was dead, I couldn't

imagine it. I tried to think about the English Channel, which, I had been told, was cold and rough. Somehow though, instead of harsh waves, grey and salty, I pictured warm ripples and sunlight.

Yes, I knew that Vienna was Hitler's, but the Danube, I imagined, was still beautiful. And surely, that was the water I kept seeing. So blue, so blue.

Van

What did I know? What do I remember? Flashbacks...fragmentary phrases...certain and uncertain feelings.....

A Saturday morning in September. I see myself, eleven years old, in that high-ceilinged barn studio on the hillside. Apprehensively, with my hands folded, I sit waiting for my first glimpse of the village artist, my new teacher Van Dyke Browne.

I wear the big-enough-to-grow-into smock my mother had made for me. On my lap—open, ready and untouched—is the beautiful new oil paint box sent from New York City by my Aunt Eleanor. Aunt Eleanor, my mother's rich, much-older sister, is paying for my lessons.

A shadow falls across my lap, blocking sun slanting from the high studio window. A smiling mountain of a man thunders down at me from what seems to be a great distance: "I'm Van, and who may you be, dear?"

He is, I am sure, the largest man I've ever seen. He has a barrel torso, arms and legs like fire logs. His head is big as a Halloween pumpkin, and from his crown, sun-ray red curls sprout in a wild, weedy way. His broad, heavy, slightly-darker red beard tangles with clumps of russet hair growing from his ears and nose so thickly I wonder how he can hear or breathe.

My parents have warned me: the class is for grown-ups, not children. I must be very polite, I am not to bother anyone. I have been admitted because last July, when Aunt Eleanor was sick in the hospital, my mother took her the spring flower pastel I did at school. Later, Aunt Eleanor called Mr. Browne— they are old friends. I can come to the morning portrait class, my mother says, but the afternoon life class "isn't appropriate." She doesn't say why.

Eager to please the first real artist I've ever met, I jump up and, as I have been taught, extend a small, polite hand. "How do you do, Mr. Browne," I begin in the best voice I can muster.

"I'm Estelle, Eleanor Rice's niece."

The giant laughs. Ignoring my hand, he reaches down and ruffles my light brown hair with rough-skinned, cucumber-size fingers. My hair, I realize, is almost as curly as his.

"Tell me," he demands in a kindly, thundering way, "have you ever painted in oils before?"

I am small for my age and flat-chested. I only come up to the middle button of his forest green, paint-stained shirt. Dropping my hand, I shake my head.

"Then let's get going."

Before I know it, Mr. Browne is sitting in my chair with my new paint box on his lap. He extracts the wooden palette and a canvas board from the grooves in the top of the box. Then he takes all the color tubes out of their neat little compartments and squeezes a rainbow arc of rich-smelling blobs onto the palette. Removing a stick of charcoal from behind one of his enormous, long-lobed ears, he asks: "Do you see this fellow sitting in front of us?"

I nod.

"That's Jim." He winks at the model, and surprisingly the man, who wears a grey suit and is about my father's age, winks back. "You're going to paint his portrait."

My mother has fed me a big breakfast, but my stomach feels empty. I'm afraid, no, certain I can't do it. Yet somehow, with Mr. Browne's russet paw kindly directing my unsure fingers, he-we-I manage to outline Jim's head, neck and shoulders.

When we finish, Mr. Browne fills the two little metal cups that clip onto my palette. One is for the yellow linseed oil, the other for turpentine. Then, bending over me so his beard tickles my forehead, he shows me how to fit my thumb into the palette and balance it almost as grandly as the grown-ups do.

I want to ask him which of my long-handled brushes to use. Just then though, the stern-looking, white-haired lady sitting beside me beckons to him silently. As he turns away, I see she is wearing a hearing aid.

There are at least twenty people in the studio besides Babs, the monitor, a high school girl I know because she lives on my block, and Lois, who is older and works with Babs. Mr. Browne is too busy to get back to me until the end of class. By that time, I've smeared a lot of paint on my canvas and quite a bit on my smock and used most of the brushes. I've given up on my blobbish attempt at a likeness of Jim, a nice-looking man, and am trying to clean up at one of the paint-spattered sinks Babs has shown me. It seems a shame to wipe the left-over colors off my palette and waste them, but how else can I slide the palette back into the paint box where it belongs?

When I go back to my easel to get my picture, Mr. Browne is there, bending over it.

"It's a beginning," he thunders in a friendly way. "You'll do a lot better next time."

"I will?" I echo, not really believing it. Then, wishing I were old enough to call him Van in the easy way the grown-ups do, I add: "Yes, Mr. Browne, I'll try."

"I haven't seen Eleanor—your aunt—in years," he tells me. "She called me. She thinks you may have talent."

I didn't know what to say. My parents always said: "Praise to the face is an open disgrace." I feel uncomfortable.

"Eleanor and I were in art school together long ago," he adds softly. "She was a beautiful woman and just married. I painted her portrait." Van pauses, a sad look shadows his big, tender, harvest-moon face. "We were all going to be the best painters in the world—back then."

There is a silence. Then Van turns to me again. Staring down from beneath the forest of eyebrows that meet over his nose, he adds: "I think you look a bit like her."

"I *do*?" I can't help bursting out. Aunt Eleanor, my mother says, hasn't been well for a long time. Her cheeks droop down at the sides of her face and jiggle when she talks, and the flesh of her ankles puffs out over the sides of her hand-made leather shoes.

"Her hair was the same color as yours—and curly," Van interjects, perhaps sensing that I don't believe him.

How can I tell him that Aunt Eleanor's hair, which has been white as long as I can remember, was chopped off in the hospital? Her thick curls are gone, and sad wisps hang straight at the back of her neck in a rough, ugly way.

Luckily perhaps, a small, dark-haired man with a pencil-thin moustache comes over to speak to Van. He has a foreign accent and dresses in the way I've always supposed an artist would. His pale, wide-collared smock is longer and fuller than mine, and a little black beret slants jauntily over his forehead.

Van introduces the man as Milo, and since I'm not sure whether the name is his first or his last (*Mr.* Milo?) I just nod. It seems there is a problem about the model for the afternoon life class. With a final, friendly wave, Van excuses himself.

Babs comes to help me unscrew my canvas from the easel. The deaf lady and some of the other grown-ups are leaving their paintings to dry on the wooden racks along the wall, but I want to take mine home to show my parents.

As we fit everything back into my new paint box, Babs tells me Milo works for Mr. Browne. "He makes appointments, keeps accounts, fills in as a model if he has to."

"I thought he was an artist."

"He is, but he can't sell anything. He doesn't paint portraits—just funny little circles and squares and triangles. He's a European refugee."

"Oh." It's after twelve. I tell Babs my mother will be waiting.

Clutching a corner of my canvas with one hand and my paint box with the other, I start up the steep hill to the road where I see our grey Chevrolet. The path is rocky and overgrown. At home, my father mows our lawn every Saturday afternoon. Here, the wildflowers bloom in all my palette's colors, and the beautiful yellow goldenrod rises high as my waist.

As I pass the old brown shingle house, I see four little red-haired children who look like Van playing on a rusty swing set. Then the back door opens and a big strawberry blonde woman calls them in for lunch. The woman, who has to be their mother, is wearing pink bedroom slippers and a blue dress torn under one arm. The children look raggedy too, and the littlest one is barefoot. Above the kitchen window, a loose drain pipe hangs down crazily.

Artists like Van, I decide, don't care about keeping things neat. Yet Aunt Eleanor, who painted a lot before she got sick, lives in a lovely-looking apartment. Maybe that's because she has maids to help her, maybe it's because she's rich—not because of selling her paintings but because of Uncle Nelson. He is the son of a famous diplomat and a diplomat himself.

My mother, like my father, is a neat and careful person. When I get to the road, she has already opened our car's trunk and spread newspapers so I can put my canvas on them. When we get home, she even helps me prop up the canvas on my desk on more newspapers. My room is a mess—I'm the only one in the family who isn't neat, but for once she doesn't ask me to pick up. She's in a hurry though: my father has to work half a day on Saturday at his office in New York, and it's time for her to go and get him at the station.

My father usually reads the war news from Europe on the train, so when he gets home, he needs a good lunch. After we eat though, my mother takes him up to my room to see my painting.

"It really doesn't look like the model at all," I admit.

"But you tried," my mother says, "you did your best."

"That's right," my father says. "Rome wasn't built in a day."

My parents believe in saying things like that. I guess I do, too. When Aunt Eleanor calls on Sunday as she always does, my mother tells her I am "working like a Trojan." When it's my turn to talk, I tell her I like oils better than pastels. I know that's what my parents would like me to say, but it's true.

The next Saturday, the model is a tall lady with brownish

57

grey hair wearing a rose-colored evening dress. Somehow—maybe I haven't cleaned my brushes enough—some green gets into the color I mix for her face, shoulders and arms. I try to cover it with white, but it doesn't look real at all. When I finish, she looks more like a vanilla frosted cookie in a red wrapper than a real person.

At the end of that morning, Babs asks me if I've seen the gallery. I don't know what she means. Taking my hand, she leads me past the studio door to a place that looks like a closet. It isn't a closet, it's a steep flight of plank board steps.

"This used to be the hayloft," she tells me as we climb past a rough wood wall of small paintings she says are Milo's. "Poor Milo," she adds, "there's so much to do here he doesn't have time to paint. Last week, when Lois got her period and wouldn't pose, he had to sit for the life class all afternoon. He hates that because he's so skinny. With his clothes off, he looks like a plucked chicken."

Do I know models for the life class are naked? Maybe I don't. I do know what periods are, my mother has warned me, but since mine haven't started yet, I feel uncomfortable. Then, I don't know why, I imagine Milo without his clothes. He looks like a grey mouse without fur. In one tiny paw he holds a miniature brush to outline the geometric shapes that float in a lonely way against the soft, cloud-like bands of color in his pictures.

When we get to the top of the steps, I can't do anything but stare. In a great and wonderful room, sun slants down from a long roof skylight onto a collection, yes, a crowd of beautiful portraits. Hanging high on the walls, standing grandly against a long row of racks, and even resting imposingly on old overstuffed chairs and couches are dozens of formally-dressed men and women in elaborate gold frames. One man in evening attire had a broad red ribbon stretched diagonally across his chest. One woman in white wears a diamond circlet on her head and is, perhaps, a princess. Other equally distinguished people—some shown full length and others only to the waist—

surround them.

For a while, I can't say anything.

"They're Van's, you know," Babs whispers, seeing how impressed I am. "Usually, when he has a big commission, he makes a copy. Then he has something to show new customers. In the winter, when he doesn't give classes because it's too snowy for people to drive up the mountainside, he works here."

"I see." I see too what it is to be a portrait painter, and at the same time, feel I may never be one. Even if I could meet such grown-ups—men and women more important than anyone I or my parents know—I wouldn't be able to make them look so beautiful.

"I've asked him to paint me," Babs says, "but I don't know if he has time—just a quick head sketch I can give my mother for Christmas."

"Babs," I can't help asking, "do you pose?"

"For the life class?"

I nod.

"Of course not. My parents wouldn't let me. Lois is out of school, you know, she's older than she looks. Her father died last year, and her mother still has young children at home."

"Oh."

Just then, as if by magic—I surely would have heard him come up the plank steps—Van is beside us. He has come, it seems, from behind one of the great racks of canvases as though stepping out of one of his own pictures. As always, he is smiling, and as he stands in one of the long bands of light that the sun makes on the floor, he looks even larger than before, his curls redder, his beard the color of fire. He almost shines, and because of it Milo, who comes behind, appears to have shrunk to a mere shadow.

"How do you like them, Estelle?" he demands, spreading his arms as if to include every canvas in the gallery. "These are my grown-up children."

"I—I—" Trying to find an answer, I finally blurt: "I look up

59

to them, but I don't believe in them."

"*Why?*"

"Because—because they're too beautiful."

Van looks surprised, then he laughs. "Too beautiful? Can anyone, particularly a woman, be *too* beautiful? Still, you're right—but my subjects don't think so."

Then, drawing me forward into his beam of light, he asks: "What do you want to be when you grow up?"

"I'm only eleven."

"And in ten years, you'll be twenty-one."

Babs and Milo nod. It's true, but perhaps because I can't imagine being that old, I shake my head. Then all three of them are waiting—I tell Van: "I want to grow up to be as big as you."

That makes everyone laugh, but I don't mean it the way it sounds. I don't want to paint people to look beautiful, but there is something about Van I do want to copy. What is it? Why do I like him? *Am* I like him? Is it just that we both have curly hair?

When Aunt Eleanor calls that Sunday, she invites us for Thanksgiving, and my mother says we'll come. When it's my turn, I tell Aunt Eleanor about Van's gallery and the portraits. Maybe my parents would like me to tell her I want to be a portrait painter, but I don't. It isn't true.

When I'm finished, there's a little pause. Then Aunt Eleanor asks: "Do you remember the portrait in my living room that hangs on the far side of the fireplace?"

I remember her living room. It faces the East River far below. On the right is a big mahogany cabinet with doors at the bottom. Inside are toys more wonderful than any I have at home. Some were my cousin Harold's before he grew up and went away to college. Others were bought by Aunt Eleanor on her trips abroad. I particularly like the little painted horse and cart from Italy and the miniature Swedish kitchen that has a tin box behind where you can put water to make the faucets run.

"Van painted me," Aunt Eleanor prompts, "when I was very young."

Finally, I have to tell her I don't remember the portrait.

"Never mind. When you come into town for Thanksgiving, I'll show it to you. You and your parents are going to keep me company. Harold is writing a paper and can't get home from Harvard, and your uncle is being sent to Europe on a special mission."

All fall, my mother drives me up the mountain every Saturday: I don't miss a class. Without a lot of success, I paint a ballet dancer in pink, an old lady in peasant costume holding a basket of fruit, a man in a black jerkin who is supposed to be Hamlet. I'm not trying to make them look beautiful—just recognizable so I won't have to explain to my parents who they are. My best, probably, is the clown in the red wig with a painted smile that makes his mouth curl up to his eyes. Without meaning to, I make the clown look a little like Van.

I plan to show the clown to Aunt Eleanor when we go for Thanksgiving, but we don't go. Aunt Eleanor has the flu. She is getting better, but she doesn't want to "give us something." She's very afraid of infections, my mother says, because long ago, her first child, a little girl, died of diphtheria.

When Thanksgiving comes, we have our turkey at home. There isn't any class that weekend, but the next Saturday is special. The first part of the specialness is—there's no model. Instead, Babs has left a little clip-on mirror on each chair. We are supposed to clip those mirrors to our easels and—paint ourselves. At first, I don't think I can do it. Then, after taking a long time to sketch everything first, I paint what my parents say looks like me. I'm not so sure. I think my face looks too thin. I look older than I am—almost grown-up.

The second thing that makes the class special is—Mr. Browne is giving us a Christmas party. After we finish the

61

self-portraits and clean up, we are invited to the gallery for punch and Christmas cookies and little sandwiches. Friends and relatives are invited. My mother comes, and my father takes an early train home from work so he can come with her. Mrs. Browne and the four red-headed children are there. The children look neater and cleaner than when I saw them in the yard, and Mrs. Browne is wearing a black skirt and a gold-sequined blouse that doesn't quite hide the bulge where she is having another baby.

After a while, when Mr. Browne is showing everyone the portraits and Milo is explaining who all the important people are who posed for them, I walk around one of the big racks of canvases nibbling a sandwich. Way back, in a place where the sun from the skylight doesn't reach, I see a door. It is slightly open. No one can see me. I tiptoe forward, open the door a little more, slip in.

The room, I realize, lies on the other side of the peaked roof and is just as big as the gallery. It has the same slanting ceiling and the same long skylight, but because this is the cold, north side of the barn, the light seems greyer, quieter, paler. The thing that isn't pale or quiet or grey though is the huge canvas sitting on the gigantic easel that has to be Van's. The five-times-as-big-as-anything-I've ever seen picture is not painted in the calm, smooth-as-cream way of the paid-for portraits in the gallery. Instead, strong colors are splashed in a wild way over the faces and bodies of what I realize is Van's portrait of himself, his wife, and his little children—all of them naked!

Without his clothes, Van looks more like a furry animal than a person. Yet he is smiling and raising his hand to wave—at whoever is looking at the picture. His wife stands beside him in the center of the canvas, and his other hand draws her close so he can raise, even offer, one of her enormous breasts.

The two little girls stand at the left beside their mother. The two little boys stand at the right, next to Mr. Browne. Like their father, the children are smiling, and no one looks at all embarrassed at being naked.

The last bite of my sandwich (ham) is in my mouth, but I have a hard time swallowing it. I cough. The voices of the people at the party are far away. I should leave, but I just stand staring.

The rough way the picture is painted—the thick, blobby smears make me think of my first portrait of Jim—brings out things it isn't polite to notice. The nipples of Mrs. Browne's breasts are brown and big as saucers. An ugly scar cuts straight down her stomach from her navel to the place where the triangle of hair begins. One of the little girls has a strawberry birthmark on her arm, and one of the little boys is cross-eyed. The hand that Van is raising to wave has dirty fingernails and paint on the palm.

Worst of all, the hair at the fork of Van's legs is dark, not red, and from it his penis sticks out for all to see, big and troubling. Rising crookedly, it seems to be pointing in my direction.

I get a terrible feeling in the pit of my stomach. Maybe I am going to be sick. It's true that I don't believe in Van's too-beautiful portraits, but I don't want to believe in this picture either. And *why* does Van, who can make people look so wonderful, wish to make himself, and his whole family, look so...so...I can't put a word to it.

Maybe because I don't know the right word, and maybe because I'm in a place I'm not supposed to be—the private studio Van must have come from the first time Babs showed me the gallery—I get scared. Backing toward the door, I stumble against a taller-than-I-am painting of a nude girl. It's Lois. She tips toward me frighteningly, not looking pale and pretty as she usually does, but sad and scrawny with her ribs sticking out and her hands clenched to fists at her sides.

Throwing my arms open, I catch her before she falls flat on her face. Her frame, though, is made of heavy, unfinished wood, and it's hard to put her back. As I struggle, the soft paint of her

63

flesh smears my smock, and her splintery frame scrapes my arms, then bangs back against the wall.

I escape as fast as I can, slamming the studio door without meaning to and veering around the high racks of polite portraits until—I almost run into the white-haired lady who has been sitting next to me every Saturday. Has she heard the noise? Does she know where I've been? No, she's deaf. I smile, trumpet, "Merry Christmas!" and find my parents.

My mother and father are talking to Van about Aunt Eleanor. He's sorry she's been sick. No one has even missed me.

Soon, it's time to go home. All the week before the party, I've been telling myself that, since I'm getting older, it might be all right if, just for once, I call him Van when we say goodbye. But when the time comes, I don't want to. Mrs. Browne gives me a candy cane to take home, but I forget and leave it behind.

Soon, we are in our grey Chevrolet, driving down the mountainside to our house, which is in a street that doesn't slope half as much. As always, my father drives, my mother sits next to him, and I sit in back. Sometimes I get mad at my parents because they always do and say the same things. I am never allowed, for instance, to sit in my mother's place in front. This time though, I don't mind.

When one of our tires goes flat on the way home and my father has to stop and fix it, I try to help him. When we finally do get home and my father says the thing he always says about how "Accidents happen even in the best of regulated families," it doesn't annoy me the way it sometimes does. Instead, I'm glad to be home, glad the portrait class is over, glad our house doesn't have any secret room nobody is supposed to see. Our house (except for my messy room with things thrown in the closet) has, as my mother says: "A place for everything and everything in its place."

Saturday afternoon, I am very tired. My mother is making

64

Christmas cookies downstairs, and I can smell them, but I just lie on my bed even though I never take naps. What am I thinking? Maybe I'm worrying about what to say to Aunt Eleanor when she calls.

I'll thank her for the lessons, of course, but if she asks if I want to take portrait lessons again in the spring—what will I tell her? I don't know, and not knowing makes me tired.

As it turns out, I don't have to tell Aunt Eleanor anything. That night, my mother sets up a card table in the living room, and we have what she calls a winter picnic supper in front of the fire my father has built in the fireplace. Those suppers with just cocoa and sandwiches and paper plates are one of the things my parents do that I like most. Our winter picnics are warm and cozy, and we don't have to have finger bowls or the linen napkins I always forget to fold and put back in my silver napkin ring.

When we are sitting down but haven't started to eat, my mother takes my hand in one of hers and my father's in the other. "We three," she says, "we're happy, aren't we?"

In the firelight I can see tears in her eyes. Sometimes, because my mother cries easily, her tears make me angry. This time though, I don't mind. But will it always be "we three," I wonder. Something tells me no. I love my parents, but maybe I'm not like them. They are neat, and I am messy. Who am I like? Can it be Van?

I'm hungry. My parents are hungry, too. Soon we have eaten all the grilled cheese sandwiches.

As we are enjoying scoops of vanilla ice cream and my mother's cookies in the shapes of stars and reindeers, there is a phone call, a sad one. It is my cousin Harold calling. Aunt Eleanor was taken to the hospital early in the morning. She had a stroke. Around noon—the very time we were at Van's party—she died.

My mother cries, I have a big lump in my throat, and my father sniffs and coughs. He tells my mother to go upstairs and rest, and he and I pick up the paper plates, put the cookies in the cookie tin and fold up the card table. Afterwards, my father lets the fire go out. We go to the glass porch and play cribbage until it's time to go to bed. Playing cribbage is another thing we always do—my father and I.

The next day, Sunday afternoon after church, my mother stays home and my father and I go to a movie about a brave sergeant in the Great War. When we come out, we hear about Pearl Harbor. Soon, we are at war ourselves.

Because of the war, my uncle can't get back to New York until the week before Christmas. Aunt Eleanor's funeral is in a big stone church on Park Avenue. I wear my let-down black velvet party dress even though it's getting tight under the arms.

We sit way in front at the beginning of the long aisle, and the dark, shiny, shut-tight coffin is beside us. While the minister talks and the organ plays, I try not to think about how Aunt Eleanor may look inside it.

When the funeral is over, we go back to the big apartment on the East River with Harold and Uncle Nelson. There, a maid in a black silk dress with white collar and cuffs passes sandwiches with the crusts cut off and slices of sponge cake on silver trays. There are things to drink, too. I have ginger ale.

Everyone is very sad and quiet, and my mother tells me it's all right if I want to go and get out toys such as the painted horse and cart and the kitchen with faucets that really work.

Somehow, I'm not interested. Instead, while the grown-ups are talking, I wander back into the long broad hall. There are bookcases there with glass doors and paintings on the walls. I'm looking at one, a big bowl of flowers I think Aunt Eleanor might have painted, when Uncle Nelson come and stands beside me.

"She painted this?" I ask.

He nods. Then he shows me other pictures by Aunt Eleanor—more flowers, a nice bowl of fruit, and finally, a small, unfinished portrait of a little girl with blonde, curly hair. "That was our little girl," he says softly. "Her name was Estelle, too."

I can't think of anything to say. Has my mother told me my dead cousin's name was the same as mine? I don't know. Finally I ask: "Is there a portrait of Aunt Eleanor?"

"Do you want to see it?" Uncle Nelson seems pleased. Quickly he leads me back through the long, dark hall.

"Mr. Browne, my portrait painting teacher, said—" I break off.

We are in the enormous living room, standing at the opposite end from where the toys are, facing a low table which holds silver candlesticks and a Chinese bowl. Above the bowl, which is wonderful, bright blue and has strange characters on it, is a life-sized portrait of a beautiful young woman with brown curls wearing a shimmering, lime-colored evening gown. The gilt-framed picture, which is so like his other works I know Van painted it, shows Aunt Eleanor half-turned away but looking back over the shoulder of her elegant, low cut dress, smiling mysteriously. To me, she looks as if she has a secret.

"We were just married then," Uncle Nelson tells me.

"Yes—" I don't know what else to say. Can I? No, I can't tell him I don't even recognize Aunt Eleanor, my aunt with white hair, puffy face and swollen ankles. All I can do is stare at the frighteningly beautiful young stranger who seems just as impossible as—what the coffin holds. Do I know what her smile means? Is it something uglier than Van's painting of himself and his family? Is it that she's having a baby—a girl who will die of diphtheria, leaving her parents because she can't breathe? Is it—?

Covering my eyes with my hands, I begin to cry in long, wrenching sobs I can't control or quiet. My father and my mother and my cousin come, and my uncle looks as if he may cry himself. The worst thing is that I don't know whether I am crying for the kind Aunt Eleanor who sent my paint box and paid for my lessons or for the beautiful stranger in Van's picture. Possibly I am also crying for the dead child—or for some-

thing else I neither know or understand. It is a long time before
I can stop crying, but when I do, my parents drive home and I
sleep most of the way.

After that, I don't see my cousin or my uncle again for years.
My cousin goes on to graduate school in California and a com-
mission in the Navy, and my uncle works in Washington all
through the war. They give up the big apartment on the East
River, and I don't know what becomes of Van's portrait of
Aunt Eleanor.

When the winter of Aunt Eleanor's death is over and spring
comes, my parents don't say anything about painting lessons,
and I don't either. Partly I don't ask because I know lessons
are expensive, and my parents, when they don't think I'm listening, talk a lot about "the mortgage" and other bills they
have to pay.

The other reason I don't raise the subject is that I don't want
to study portrait painting any more. I want the impossible—to
enroll in the life class on Saturday afternoons. Yes, I've painted
portraits over the winter—one of my mother and one of my
father, and they like them. The trouble is: I'm tired of making
people look their best. Another winter canvas, a self-portrait,
shows pimples and the way molars pushing up in the back of
my mouth are making my front teeth crooked.

My last portrait, painted at the beginning of April, is completely crazy. It's Van, but his whole face is covered with green
leaves and branches. You can still see his nose and mouth, and
his eyes, peering out, follow you. My viridian green runs out
before I can finish, but when I show this one to my parents, my
mother recognizes him. My father, making a joke, calls it "The
Green Van." Or does he say "The Green Pan?"

I don't show everything to my parents any more. Hidden in
the back of my closet where I'm pretty sure my mother won't
find it is a private sketchbook I've started. In it, I've drawn
myself in charcoal—without clothes. Naturally, I don't make a

painting from it. Where could I put the canvas to dry? Besides, I have other things on my mind. I'm not the smallest girl in my class any more. In the fall, I'll be starting Junior High School. At the end of the summer, I actually persuade my mother to buy me a bra.

When you're eleven or so—I turn twelve that August—it's hard to imagine how much things will change. People you expect will go on being part of your life disappear, and sometimes you don't see them again for years—or ever.

Later, when I get to be twenty-one years old and am going to art school in New York City, I do see my cousin, who's become an engineer, and my uncle, who's retired to a smaller apartment on the East River. By this time, my father has died and my mother has sold our house and moved away, and I hardly ever see anyone from home any more.

I guess that's why I'm so surprised when, coming out of the Museum of Modern Art one bitterly cold, snowy day just before Christmas, I run into Van Dyke Browne.

He has changed: his bushy red curls and beard have turned a brilliant, Santa Claus white. Perhaps because I have grown up to be almost as tall as my father, he doesn't seem quite as enormous as he did when I was eleven. Naturally, he doesn't recognize me, but when I mention Aunt Eleanor, he remembers. I tell him I am studying painting, and he tells me he has just been commissioned to do the official portrait of The Governor. That's good, because three of his children—he has six—are in college.

I wonder about the cross-eyed boy and the girl with the strawberry birthmark, but I certainly don't ask. He is hurrying to the opening of a show by Milo, who has married Lois. Geometric abstractions, I realize, are at last in vogue.

It is snowing heavily. As we shake hands, a rising wind flings wet, white blobs in our faces. A crown of snow is settling on his head. I see that someone, surely his wife, has pinned a bough of holly on his breast.

"Good-bye and good luck," he intones kindly, turning away. "Keep painting," he calls back over a massive shoulder. On the back of his greenish-grey greatcoat lie mounds of snow like folded wings. A fog of furiously falling flakes whirls between us. He is disappearing.

Do I know what Van taught me when I was eleven? Do I remember? Maybe. Maybe not everything. Still, on the strength of it, I could follow him into the maelstrom of snow like a votary.

But I don't. I stand there. The time has come. Loudly, boldly, one-artist-to-another, I call after him into the wind: "Good-bye...Merry Christmas...*Van*."

His Ambition

I never really cared for him. Who can say why? Perhaps it was because Norman was so pale and serious. Perhaps it was because his hands trembled even if he was only passing me a drink of water.

I was nineteen, and I liked to laugh. I guess that was a good thing—it was a funny summer. The war was over, but my father was still in Germany with the Army of Occupation, and my mother, well, she'd had to go away for a while.

The twins—Ron and Rob—and I didn't tell everyone, but she'd had a nervous breakdown in March, in the middle of my first year away at college. I almost chucked my courses then and called it quits, but everyone said I should stick it out. So I did—even though I was just grinding through. Nothing there really interested me, but I couldn't figure out what else did.

The twins, who were in their last year of high school, insisted they could keep the house going alone. They did a good job of it, but of course Aunt Mush—yes, my father's sister, she was plump and white haired and that was what we'd always called her—lived right across the street. She and Uncle Bucky—they had never had children—were glad to have the boys come over for dinner almost every night.

When I came home in June, everything was fine. Even the spare room where Mother had slept after Dad couldn't get leave to come home for Christmas had been cleaned. All the scraps of colored cotton which she said she was saving for a quilt but which, at the end, she was only cutting into smaller and smaller pieces, were gone.

The sewing machine—the one with which she'd tried to stitch her fingers together the night Bucky had to call the ambulance—had been sent to Bundles for Britain. It was lucky that Bucky had gone into insurance after losing most of the calf of one leg to a Doberman someone had left with him. He was used to blood.

71

Another good thing was that the blinds my mother had kept shut even in broad daylight had been taken down. There were new, white, clean tie-back curtains billowing at the windows.

But to get back to Norman, who I hoped didn't know about any of this, or, if he did, would be too polite to mention it, Norman had been writing to me at college. The letters and packages came at least once a month, sometimes oftener.

The letters told about his job at the bank downtown where his father ran the trust department and how—he always underlined and capitalized it—he was there "ONLY TEMPORARILY." That was because, as soon as he could save enough money, he was going to "START ART SCHOOL." But Norman's letters, which also told about the one weekend each month when he went and trained with "THE NATIONAL GUARD," were nothing compared to his packages.

Each one was elaborately wrapped—sometimes with sheets of wood on both sides for protection. Most contained pen and ink drawings, and there was no doubt he had spent hours on them. The biggest one—I tacked it up over my bed—was a castle so high its battlements were among clouds and eagles.

Another, which was almost as big, showed a quiet steam, a bridge, and a little grotto with a romantic bench beside a waterfall. It was inscribed in the corner: "TO MY MATILDA." Yes, that was my name.

Norman's style matched the subjects he chose. It was elaborate. He had pens that did curlicues, French curves, and all sorts of feathery strokes. His cross hatching was so intricate that it suggested grass tangles, or perhaps, threads from cloth torn or scissored impatiently.

The same love of detail showed up in the delicate little objects of wood that came when he wasn't sending letters or drawings. The best one was a miniature violin he had carved, stained and embellished with gold lines. It didn't have a bow, but it did have the proper number of strings.

Naturally, after all those missives, I felt obligated to be very nice to Norman that Saturday in June when he came to pick me up for our first date since Christmas. I put on my best dress— even though we were only walking down to the village for a double feature. I had primed the twins—who were good kids— and they asked him so many questions about The National Guard before we left that we missed most of the newsreel.

Afterwards, when we were having sodas at the drug store, he invited me to go sketching with him the next weekend at the State Park. When I asked how we would get there, he said his father allowed him to use the car sometimes on Sunday afternoons. "You still have your sketch books, don't you?" he asked as though giving a military command. "You must bring every one of them." Norman talked that way sometimes; it was the influence of The National Guard. I was used to that sort of thing from my father, so it didn't bother me.

Nevertheless, he had touched a sore point. Norman and I had first gotten to know each other in high school art class, so he knew I could draw and had, in fact, won a second place red ribbon to his first place blue in the graduation art show in the gymnasium.

What he didn't know though was that my mother, whom we'd never mentioned, had cut up a lot more than quilting squares. She'd torn up all my paintings and sketch books, and she'd also clawed off a lot of the wall paper in the third floor bathroom—which the twins never used, so they didn't notice it until the end.

Although Ron, who was usually the leader, had gotten rid of most of the evidence—she had even cut holes in people's clothes. The canvas apron that Dad wore for barbecues in the back yard, for instance, had a cut out right below the waist that looked like a flash of lightning. In my closet, since I'd taken most of my clothes to college, she'd taken down the quilt from the top shelf and—well, it wasn't bad enough to throw out. Aunt Mush, who didn't see well, had stitched the corners Mother had clipped like a dog's ears, but the quilt, which was

73

back on the shelf, still snowed down feathers when I shut the closet door.

In spite of all that, I didn't want to say no to Norman, so I agreed—remarking casually that I'd left my sketch books at college and would have to buy more. He barely noticed, because by that time we were back at my front stoop, and he was trying to kiss me for the first time.

How can you explain why you don't want to kiss someone? Was it that his hair was the color of a paled-out egg yolk? Was it that his lips were so thin? Was it that his teeth were very small and white and his eyelashes so pale and fine you could scarcely see them?

All I can say is that there was something about him that was like the art he had sent me. If, on resisting him by placing my hands against his shoulders, I had discovered he was carved from wood, I wouldn't have been surprised. He seemed all lines and whorls, rigidly incised.

Be that as it may, he wasn't discouraged because I'd drawn away from him. The next week, when we got home from the State Park after dark in his father's car, he tried again. Maybe because I'd truly enjoyed the sketching—I'd made more drawings of trees than he had—anyway, I sat there with him for a while until he had me pressed against the back of the seat. When he kissed me, I thought about licking an envelope. White. Legal size.

Then, luckily, I saw the twins, who were working that summer as lifeguards at the pool in Memorial Park, coming home from Aunt Mush's where they were learning to play bridge. It was my excuse to head up the walk, but of course Norman came with me.

He asked me if I would be his date for what was for him the big event of the summer—The National Guard Fourth of July Dance at the Armory in the State Capital. It was formal, and afterwards we would go with friends of his to a very nice nightclub—the Blue Rooster. Before the war, when my mother and father liked to go dancing on Saturday nights, it was the place they usually went.

Naturally, I accepted. I wasn't looking forward to the Armory, but I wanted to see the Blue Rooster.

The next week—it was mid-June—I found myself a job selling encyclopedias. It wasn't that we had to pinch every penny. Uncle Bucky, who was managing everything, said that we children, and in particular, my mother, were very "well covered." That was an insurance term, but somehow, it made me think of the quilt in the closet.

Anyway, I liked the idea of having some money of my own—just in case I decided to do something different and not go back to college at all. I took the encyclopedias seriously and made a lot of calls—and a respectable number of sales.

Perhaps I was out working when the phone rang, but in any case, I didn't hear from Norman for several weeks. Aunt Mush told me she had seen him coming out of the bank one evening with a girl, but I said it was probably his older sister, who worked there too. Aunt Mush said she thought he's had his arm around her, but I discounted it. After all, the lenses of her glasses were like Coke bottle bottoms.

When Norman finally did call again, it was to arrange for picking me up at five o'clock on The Fourth and to ask what color dress I was wearing—for the corsage. I'd even forgotten it was formal, but I remembered that the sky colored dress I'd worn to Senior Prom was still hanging in the garment bag in the back of my closet, so I told him "Blue."

We didn't talk long, he had to go somewhere, but he did explain that he'd been staying late at the bank. "We're all very busy," he said, "it's the end of the fiscal year."

Right after we hung up, the phone rang again. The twins were across the street, so I answered. It was a doctor from The Hills, which was where my mother was. He asked for my father, but when I said he was still in Berlin, he told me my mother was a lot better. They were having a family day on The

75

Fourth, and we would be allowed to visit. Perhaps—if she kept on improving—we could bring her home for an hour or two.

Now, believe it or not, I hadn't thought a lot about my mother since she'd been gone. Aunt Mush and Bucky had been several times and said she was well taken care of but wasn't ready to see us children. I accepted that. Ron and Rob and I agreed that she would get better, but we had gotten used to Dad's absence, and now we were getting used to hers. The memories of all five of us being together for holidays like Fourth of July were blurred. They were part of our childhoods.

The next day, though, the possibility of just such an occasion began to seem less distant. We got a V-Mail letter from Dad saying he could be home before Labor Day. He was leaving the Army and, in a few months, he was going to go back to being a dentist downtown. He didn't say anything about Mom, but he said he hoped we would all be together again by Christmas, and you could read between the lines.

"What will it be like?" Ron asked me that afternoon. He was using a knife edge to try to remove the thumb tack he'd picked up in the sole of his sneaker. I rescued the knife—it was one of the twelve ivory handled ones which Mother, when she was all right, had always kept in the velvet-lined box in the dining room sideboard.

With the screwdriver I gave him instead, Ron extracted the tack and then—kids are crazy—started using it to dig chocolate chips out of the cookies he was eating. After I put a stop to that, Rob, who'd been out mowing the front lawn, came for lemonade and tracked in moist lumps of grass all over the red and white squares of the kitchen linoleum.

I don't know what was wrong with me—after all, he was *doing* the lawn, and I'd only had to ask him *once*—but I started to rip apart the old dish cloth I happened to be holding. I screamed at Rob—and Ron too—and told them to get out of the house.

Almost immediately, I apologized. We all sat down together

on the back porch and finished the lemonade. The problem, I guess, was that all of us were pretty much O.K. about the way things *were*—but we couldn't face up to anything *more*. It was like trying to put a broken pitcher together again. Rob, I noticed but didn't mention, had been mowing the lawn in criss-cross swatches instead of up and down. My hands, I realized when I rinsed off the lemonade stickiness afterwards, had been cut to bleeding by the dish cloth's strings, and there were half moon nail marks on my palm.

On the Fourth of July, our main problem was scheduling. The Hills was fifty miles away, and it would take an hour to get there. Then, if she seemed more or less all right, we had to get Mom into the car—Bucky was driving his big station wagon with the automatic door locks—bring her home for a holiday picnic fixed in advance, and then, after we'd eaten, take her back there and come home again. All this, hopefully, would happen well before five o'clock when Norman would come marching up the walk in his tuxedo.

It didn't quite work out.

My alarm went off at seven—just when some kids down the block lit their first firecracker. By eight, I'd eaten and cut up hard-boiled eggs into the cooked potatoes for salad. Then I got the ham ready to go into the oven—we'd decided against cooking hot dogs on skewers or anything like that. The ham, after it cooled a little, could be sliced in advance.

At nine-thirty, the boys were fed and ready the way we'd planned, and Bucky was turning the station wagon around in our driveway. Aunt Mush had forgotten to fill the tank, but there was a place open out on the main road, even though it was a holiday. We got to the Hills—which didn't look like a prison the way I'd imagined—but was just a collection of old fashioned brick buildings set amidst big trees.

The place looked almost like a campus, and in fact, when they finally brought her out to us, wearing a white dress I didn't recognize, I almost felt *I* was the mother who had come to pick *her* up at college or somewhere. For maybe the first time too, I realized I was quite a lot taller than she. Her hair had become streaked with grey, but it wasn't so much that she seemed old to me, just *little*.

Anyway, the beginning of the plan went like clockwork. She got into the car—sitting between Rob and Ron in the third seat. Every time I looked back at them she was quiet, maybe even a bit dreamy—but smiling.

Traffic we hadn't expected delayed us on the way home. I could smell the ham by the time we pulled into our driveway, but it wasn't really burned. The twins walked her around in the yard while I sliced it. I hid the big knife on the bottom shelf behind the flour and sugar canisters.

We ate our fill. I had to cut up Mother's meat, but she didn't seem to mind. She nodded when we said things to her. I think she knew who we all were. Everyone began to relax. Things didn't start to go wrong until almost three o'clock. That was when we couldn't find Mother.

How did it happen? Naturally, we all had our eyes on her. But Aunt Mush had gone across the street to get a chocolate cake because the twins had eaten the one I'd made, and Bucky, who had drunk several beers, was stretched out in Dad's old lawn chair with his eyes not really shut, but almost.

Mother, who had behaved like a guest in her own house all along—pointing to the new curtains and to the snapdragons I'd planted—had been sitting on the steps of the back porch, watching Ron and Rob toss a baseball back and forth. I was keeping my eye on things from the window over the sink—I was doing the dishes. She seemed to be enjoying the sun, but I heard her say the same word several times. It was "mouth."

I decided it would be a good ideal to give her a drink of water, so I went to the cupboard to get a clean glass. When I got back to the sink, the sun was on the step—but Mother wasn't.

78

At first I thought she might have strolled around the corner of the house to the car—it *was* time to go. When I dashed out and found she wasn't there—or anywhere—I screamed.

Somebody let off some cannon rockets up the street at just that moment, and Bucky jumped out of his chair as if the war had started all over again. Aunt Mush came running so fast with the cake that she smeared chocolate frosting all over the front of her dress, and the twins rushed inside—searching the house from cellar to attic.

We had hidden the scissors and pins and razors after breakfast, and all the kitchen knives except the big one I mentioned were tucked away underneath the garbage bags. My stomach— which was full—turned over though when I remembered the ivory handles knives in the dining room.

I ran to check them. They were all there. Bucky was using the phone on the table in the hall. He was calling the police.

The boys went all through the house again and so did Bucky. The police were slow in coming—I suppose because of the holiday. Then, I thought of the little space in my closet beyond where the dress bag hung. I ran up alone, and yes, there was a pair of white shoes on the floor, way back, which had feet in them.

Somehow, I couldn't speak, I couldn't call to her. I just slid the open dress bag forward very gently and found her standing there politely, licking her lips. She looked as if she had been waiting for someone to help her out all along. After I'd called to the twins and Bucky I wondered about the quilt. But when I glanced back as we were leading her downstairs, I saw that it was still folded on the top shelf.

We explained to the police, and that was all right, but just as they were leaving—the whole search had taken a lot longer than we'd realized—I saw Norman pull up in his father's car. So, just as he was coming up the walk in his tuxedo carrying my corsage in a white florist's box, the police were going down it.

Aunt Mush took charge then and there—I was crying. "You stay here," she told me. "we'll get your mother to The Hills." Then she told Bucky to back up the station wagon.

The boys—who were standing in the front porch with Mom, one on each side—started to maneuver her down the front steps. When she saw Norman though—he had stepped aside, behind the hydrangea bush—she stopped dead.

I wouldn't have believed she'd remember him, but maybe the art prizes came back to her. She said: "Hello, Norman." It was her first complete sentence all day.

Stiff as a soldier, he nodded in reply. "Good evening."

The twins were at her elbows. They were propelling her toward the car very quickly without actually carrying her. As they reached the back door of the station wagon, which Aunt Mush was holding open, she turned back towards Norman and said: "You're an artist."

"Yes'm," he answered woodenly, in a way that was as formal as a salute.

"Artists," she said very clearly and primly as she toed one of the white shoes I had seen in the closet inside the station wagon, "copulate a lot."

Maybe he answered her, but I'm quite sure he didn't. All I remember is that I ran inside—and upstairs to my room. After I'd lain on the bed for a while with my eyes shut, listening to the station wagon back out over the gravel and turn down the block, I blew my nose and got up. Then I went to the front window in what had always been my parents' room and called down to Norman, whose black trousered legs and black, polished shoes I could see from above—he was sitting in the porch rocker with the corsage box on his lap. I said I was going to get cleaned up and wouldn't be long.

I had intended to take my dress out of the closet and press it before he arrived. Instead, I was in such a hurry that I just snatched it out of the bag and put it on. In the hall, when I was pirouetting before the mirror at the foot of the attic steps to make sure that my petticoats didn't show, I got one more un-pleasant surprise.

The hole in the skirt wasn't as big as it might have been, but it was right in the middle of the back. My mother hadn't had scissors, she hadn't even used her nails. Instead, she had simply bitten a mouth-sized hole in the blue net. The hole was still a little damp at the edges—to chew it hadn't been easy. When I opened the door to the closet again—the feathers came out in my face as usual—I found the wadded, saliva-covered frag-ment on the closet floor.

Luckily—if you can use the word in a situation like that—I found some thread that almost matched. The skirt was full. The place showed—but only a little.

The dinner dance at the Armory was a blur to me. I can't remember whether I ate or not. When we went back and forth to the dance floor, I twisted and turned so that he wouldn't see the tear.

Even at the Blue Rooster, a much larger place than I had expected, I was still edgy. Afterwards, maybe because I'd let him order a drink for me, I began to relax.

When I got home and parked in front of my house, the hall light was on and that was all. That meant the twins had gone to bed. Bucky's station wagon was parked in his driveway.

Norman, of course, hadn't mentioned my mother all evening. Instead, he repeated the things he'd written in letters about his ambition to become an artist. In the fall, he told me conclu-sively, taking his key out of the ignition, he was going to begin "THE BIG CHANGE" and start "A VERY GOOD ART SCHOOL" at night.

The street light was half a block down, and when he leaned forward to press me against the back of the seat again, the yellow dimness made him look more like wax than wood. That time, I didn't press my palms against his shoulders, I just stared at the round light in the brown plush ceiling of his father's car.

It wasn't on. There was a satisfaction, I was discovering, in doing what you don't want to do.

After that, I didn't see Norman again until the end of the summer. Maybe it was because of my mother, maybe it wasn't. Either way, it didn't matter. Nothing did.

In fact, I was sort of like a zombie for the rest of that summer until the day my father arrived—looking—well, looking wonderful. Bucky and Mush gave a party that night, and no one suggested bringing my mother, for we knew by then she would be at The Hills longer than we'd thought.

I was all right that night. I was all right the next morning, but at lunch—we were eating egg salad sandwiches at the kitchen table—I collapsed.

I went to my room and stayed there for three days, crying a lot of the time. The men—the twins seemed older and more responsible now that Dad was back—were very nice to me. Finally, the last evening, when I smelled dinner cooking and got hungry and came down dressed, Norman was in the living room chatting with my father.

He had just dropped by, he said, and, because there were military things to talk about, my father invited him for dinner and he stayed.

He suggested a ride after that, but I demurred. So we just sat on the porch until the others went inside. Finally, after the streetlight went on down the block, he told me he was getting married. It was a secretary at the bank. Somehow, he had thought he ought to—

I wasn't sorry a bit, but I felt sad when he told me that the rest of his plans had changed. Norman—who seemed more than ever like one of his own drawings—pale and precise— wasn't going to be an artist after all. He was going to stay on at the bank, and at night he would be studying business. It was, of course, what his father had wanted all along.

Finally—he was standing on the bottom step, I was on the top one—he told me quietly: "She's on the way already."

Aunt Mush, who saw more than you expected, confirmed it to me in the fall. She had seen the girl—the same one she had noticed with him in June—and she was well, bunching her coat around her waist.

Later, I saw her myself. She was almost as pale as Norman and had intricate blonde curls. Her name was Verna Lou.

I have a very poor memory. Truthfully, there are a lot of things I forget. I think though that by the time my mother came home—not that year but the next—Norman's wife was already expecting again. By that time—my mother had been retrained in therapy to be Dad's dental assistant (they said she was good with her hands)—I wasn't going to college any more.

Instead, as I told Norman late one afternoon when I ran into him as he was leaving the bank, I was in "A VERY GOOD ART SCHOOL." I had new sketch books. I was going to be an illustrator of children's books.

Norman congratulated me—he still had that formal, military way about him. He was still in the National Guard.

When I got home—I was just sitting in my room waiting for my mother to call me for dinner—I noticed his little violin on my bookcase. I picked it up. I saw the precision of the carving, the intricacy of the painted gold decoration. After dinner—a meal at which everything struck me as funny, I laughed so much my father had to ask me to stop—I went and got the violin and gave it to Mother, who liked well-cut things.

After all, I didn't need the violin to remind me of that summer. Yes, Verna Lu had his baby, but I had HIS AMBITION.

A Matter of Money

We couldn't afford it, but I went anyway. My mother, recently widowed, paid somehow for summer school at Harvard.

I was to make up for the Greek course I had failed at Wellesley by taking French and, on the side, auditing a course in poetry. I took the cheapest accommodations—four flights up in one of the oldest residence halls. My father had died the winter before, and I still had two more years before I would graduate.

I shared a suite with a blonde appropriately named Honey. After the first week of the seven week session, she seldom slept there. Her lover was a quarterback named Have—short for Haverford. If he had a first name, she didn't use it.

Once, lying on her bureau, which was right beside mine, I saw a penciled note from him which read: "Honey, I'm hot for your body."

The words stuck in my mind, but they were as remote as the irregular verbs I was struggling to commit to memory. I was a virgin. I observed such things as a pedestrian peering into a vast greenhouse from a snowy sidewalk—sensing the heat without feeling it warm my flesh.

I was there to supplement the meager course I'd had in high school by learning advanced French in seven weeks, but of course I wanted other things. I was intellectually greedy, checking books out of the Widener Library by the armload, auditing other courses and taking voluminous notes, and spending afternoons in the Lamont Library where they had records. There, in a pale oak paneled upstairs room, you could sit in a comfortable chair and listen to T.S. Eliot, Wallace Stevens, e.e. cummings rendering their poetry repeatedly.

At the end of the first week, I ventured into the Romanesque recesses of H. H. Richardson's Sever Hall. The creaking old amphitheater was crammed to the rafters. Professor F. O. Matthiessen was grey as a stick. His suit hung loosely on his lean frame; he was slow in climbing to the podium, and some-time, his voice quavered. It wasn't every day, any more, that you could hear him lecture on T.S. Eliot.

When Matthiessen explained "The Love Song of J. Alfred Prufrock," there wasn't a sound except the creaking of the wooden seats, which had arms you pulled up for writing. Of course, the place wasn't air-conditioned. In the midst of "No! I am not Prince Hamlet," I noticed beads of sweat standing on the forehead of the student diagonally in front of me—a man whose blond hair rose straight up from his head in an over-grown crew cut.

The next week, after an hour of "Sweeney Among the Night-ingales." he and I began to talk. Abbott ended up walking me back to my dormitory, and then we sat for a while on one of the benches the architect had incorporated amidst orientalizing Vic-torian columns at the entrance.

He was from Boston and was going to be a senior at Harvard. His last name was the same as one of the university buildings, but it didn't occur to me then to make the connection—let alone see that it was important.

We talked about poetry. Everyone in his family did some-thing else—I forget what—but he said that Eliot and Pound and Wallace Stevens were what he cared about. As he said it, new beads of sweat stood out on his forehead, and his hands shook slightly. The windblown way his hair rose improbably from his crown, I decided, made me think of Mercury, the her-ald of the gods.

"Let us go then, you and I/ When the evening is spread out against the sky," he intoned abruptly, staring fixedly into the ivy which had almost obscured the pseudo-Moorish column capital above my head. "Like a patient etherized upon a table;" he went on in a rasping, unsettled voice, giving me the rest of the first stanza of Prufrock.

Seeing what it meant to me, he switched grandly and sud-denly to "We are the hollow men," which he rendered with a bit less assurance. Just as he was hesitating over "Shape without form, shade without colour, / Paralysed force," his hand tightening on the black, cloth-bound volume of the *Collected Poems* which I knew he would not open, the bells chimed.

Scorning the steps, Abbott leaped from the porch to the ground and waved. "See you at Matthiessen's," he called back in a tone that suggested we would be meeting at a sacred shrine.

He was gone before I could answer. No matter. It was clear that the course which I had tried out once the previous week in French Symbolist Poetry would have to be eliminated because it met at the same time. Already, I would have followed Abbott anywhere.

But, after thinking about him all weekend in the library, I only saw him from a distance during the first days of the third week of the session. On Monday, he was alone in the first row at Mattiessen's feet and I didn't dare join him. On Tuesday, he was in the top row, crammed amidst friends.

In the meantime, at the intersection of two paths that crossed into the open, tree-shaded space in front of Widener, I ran into Cass again.

I had met Cass Freshman year at a Wellesley-Harvard mixer—one of those unexplainable times when everything clicks. For no reason—I had long, reddish brown hair but was far from the prettiest—the men cut in on me one after another. I laughed and whirled and smiled at all of them, but the one I ended up with was Cass, a twenty year old Harvard pre-med.

Three months later, he asked me to marry him. "It's not an immediate thing," he informed me. "It would have to be after graduation—mine, that is. We'd probably have to live in some hole in Cambridge while I work my way through, at least until I do my residency. You could finish up at Radcliffe I suppose, but it doesn't matter. I'll find a way to take care of you—I wouldn't want my wife to work."

It was my first proposal, and that was exciting. Somehow though, I had the feeling I was engaged to something else. Of course, even then I knew girls who were engaged or actually married—a junior who had just gotten her ring, a senior who was living off campus and pregnant. Yet, at the center of such situations, there was always a core of sadness. Beyond the dresses, the flowers, and the brave smiles of the one so singled out, there was always the suggestion that her feelings were somehow more delicate than those of the man of her choice— usually a shadowy, logical minded, even threatening figure.

Anyway, I had marshaled convincing reasons why I couldn't become engaged to Cass. The best was religion. I was a believer, in a plain, Protestant way, and Cass was an agnostic who thought the philosophies of Bertrand Russell and Alfred North Whitehead were enough.

It was a difference I was able to make a lot of, and after Christmas Sophmore year, we decided to stop seeing each other. That meant no more Saturday night dances at Harvard or kisses afterward standing in the snow outside my dormitory door.

Maybe I thought there would be someone else right away. There wasn't. In the spring, I joined Christian Youth Volunteers and attended Sunday evening meetings at a church in Boston. For at least a month—before exams came and I got busy—I worked an afternoon a week at a clinic for cerebral palsy victims.

Even before summer vacation though, I saw good works didn't suffice. I guess that was why I couldn't eat lunch on Wednesday—the day I went to Matthiessen's class early, determined to talk to Abbott again. Sickeningly, I failed to find him—but then he came in late and sat down next to me.

"I'm *obligated*," Abbott told me in a harsh, throaty whisper that recalled the voice he'd used for Prufrock, "to spend weekends with my mother in Newport. She's a widow—my father died at Christmas—*you know*—"

He paused as Matthiessen passed out reading lists for Laforgue and other French influences on Eliot, then gasped for breath and added in an unforgettable, strangled way: "Thursday night there's a symphony concert by the Charles River—will you come with me?"

I nodded. That was all I could do. Matthiessen was on the podium, opening the *Collected Poems*. It was one of his best lectures, but I remembered almost nothing of it afterwards.

Of course, Thursday suited me fine, because I'd already promised to see Cass Saturday "for the last time."

"I'm virtually engaged," Cass had explained to me after we'd crossed the Yard together and seated ourselves on a funereal, white marble bench behind Sever Hall across the street from the Fogg Museum. "Her name is Barbara, and she's taking an advanced course in nursing administration this summer in California."

Getting out his wallet, Cass displayed a blurry black and white snapshot of a girl who looked more buxom and jolly than I would ever be. He was willing to see me Saturday night, "Just to catch up on what has happened to you."

Then, hurrying to a class, he added, almost furtively: "I'm not in the dorm anymore. I have my own apartment. It's just a little place—not far from the Yard."

Thursday night with Abbott was virtually perfect. I was an ignoramus about a lot of things, and classical music was one of them. But just to sit by the river as the sun set and the violins began....

Perhaps Abbott didn't know a lot more than I did about music—even though he told me that his parents had always had a box at the Symphony. In any case, it wasn't what we talked about.

During intermission, when we walked near the water—or paced, in Abbott's case—he recited "The Hollow Men" all the way through with a sureness that suggested he had boned up on it. He rendered "This is the way the world ends" in a theatrical whisper, and repeated "Not with a bang but a whimper" several times.

Then, while we were driving back—he was using a comfortable sedan that belonged to his mother—he revealed that he was composing a four poem sequence that was "a little like Eliot's Quartets," but of course "totally different in feeling."

Finally, when we said good-bye after midnight on the steps of my dormitory, his body brushed against mine. It wasn't like a kiss, it was like receiving an electric charge.

But the next week, except for the Friday we ran into each other in the hall after class, I scarcely saw Abbott. That morning, he paused only for a moment to lean down towards me—he was over six feet not counting his upstanding hair. "I'm in the midst of my quartets," he whispered darkly, somehow reminding me of a pale falcon, "—but *they're not going well.*" Reaching for my hand, he grasped it painfully with damp, clenching fingers—and then broke away.

I myself had never tried to write anything that wasn't an assignment, but I sympathized. It seemed even then that some fateful force might separate us, but the mere possibility made me willing to devote the rest of my life to him.

Dreamily, as I climbed the four flights to my rooms, I pictured myself married to Abbott and living in a cottage on the Charles which was picturesquely isolated but nevertheless not far from Widener Library. I was from Central New York State, and to live by water struck me as unusual, romantic.

Before Abbott finished his poems though, something else happened to me. The previous Saturday night, Cass had taken me to dinner at a small restaurant, and then, as a surprise, to a performance of "Six Characters in Search of an Author."

By the time the play was over, I was sleepy and slightly confused. Pirandello made me feel everything was uncertain. People I myself might know, I realized, were not fixed entities, but rather, variable and endlessly contradictory.

Maybe that was why, when Cass decided on the spur of the moment to show me his apartment—which was on the way back from the theatre—we turned immediately to the couch. It was the only sizeable piece of furniture there besides his desk. Serving also as his bed, it was shrouded in a loose flowered cover which, I soon learned, smelled musty. For, almost immediately, we found ourselves lying on it stuck together like postage stamps.

In all the months that Cass and I were serious about each other and almost engaged, we had seldom been alone—unless you count a few minutes in the dorm rooms he shared with three others or the end of the evening good-byes at my Wellesley dormitory when a lot of other couples were kissing good-night.

So for fifteen minutes—truthfully nearer to twenty—we lay fully clothed, stiff as pokers, kissing until the dark stubble of his beard reddened my chin. For that whole time, his arms encircled my shoulders and mine his. We were like statues on a tomb.

Finally Cass stood up, stumbling in the frayed edge of the thin dust-colored rug as he did so. Then, towering over me— he was not as tall as Abbott but heavier with dark, well combed hair—he spoke quickly, almost angrily.

"There's a dichotomy between what I told you before and the way I've acted. To say what I've said again would be a tautology, yet perhaps in this case it's reasonable to be redundant. It may seem a *non sequitur*, but I'm going to marry Barbara."

Cass had always liked to lecture. For a minute while he talked, I just lay there on my back with my dress pressed into still warm wrinkles against my hips and legs, staring at the ceiling. The ceiling was beige, stippled plaster like the walls, and it contained a brass, three bulb fixture in which one bulb was dead.

Then realizing how warm the room was, I sat up and asked Cass to turn on the small revolving fan on his desk. After that, I asked for a drink of water. While I drank it, he showed me the pictures of Barbara he had on his bureau.

It wasn't until after he'd walked me back to the dormitory

at midnight that I realized I'd never told him about what I'd done since Christmas. Somehow, I wasn't sorry. There was nothing to tell except for the courses I'd taken spring semester and the volunteers. And I was tired of the volunteers, I realized. I didn't want to offer myself calmly along with the others, I wanted to be swept away.

I climbed to the rooms, and Honey was there for once, sitting in the open window wearing an eyelet trimmed, white nightgown. She had a book in her hand, but she wasn't reading. Her summer course was "Introduction to Sociology." And it didn't take up a lot of her time.

"You're late," she commented, "did you have a date?"

I nodded. "Where's Have?"

"We quarreled."

"He'll come back."

"He's only the second man I've—well—you know," she confided. "The other was a long time ago. I was only sixteen."

Of course she expected me to tell her something in return, but I couldn't. What was there to say? How could I explain that I was ready, yes, desperately eager to follow Abbott to the ends of the earth—but that I had just been lying with Cass in a steamy embrace?

It wasn't logical, so I muttered in my newfound French: *"Honi soit que mal y pense."* Sometimes, it was better to allow people to think the worst.

Then, after I'd gotten into the top bunk of the double decker bed and turned out the light, I thought to ask: "What did you quarrel about?"

"It wasn't exactly a quarrel," she told me. "It's that his father is the head of a major corporation—and mine isn't."

"Oh—" My eyes were already shut, I didn't ask more. My father had been a small town lawyer, my mother and my brother, a freshman in high school, still lived in the same house we'd had before my father got cancer. But now, my mother worked and rented my room in the winters to a girl who went to the community college across town.

Sleep came almost immediately, but I was vaguely aware when Honey crawled into the bottom bunk. Then softly, as if from a distance, I heard her crying.

The next week, as if pressed by and invisible mold, my summer took final shape. Thursday, I went again with Abbott to a concert by the Charles. The only differences were that they played Schubert instead of Brahms and that he took me dancing afterwards at a place in Boston where there was a jazz band in a dimly lighted room behind the bar.

Abbott didn't recite poetry while he danced, but he breathed heavily, sometimes closing his eyes in a way which suggested he was working on a difficult line in his quartets—about which he made me promise not to ask.

Several weeks later, after the final concert of the season, Abbott presented me with the typed manuscripts in a gold tooled, green Morocco folder imprinted with his initials. The poems, which were moving but lugubrious, were mainly about time. Life, according to Abbott, went very fast in places like "Beacon Hill" (the title of the first quartet) and "Newport" (the title of the fourth).

There was more, of course, but the manuscripts disappeared when my mother cleaned my room after Christmas. The portfolio, though, stayed for a long time in my top bureau drawer beneath silk scarves, never used handkerchiefs sent as birthday gifts by aunts, and sachets which retained only faint reminders of their former fragrances. Even then, I realized such leather was very costly.

The other part of the summer's pattern was seeing Cass on Saturdays, and, as August approached, Mondays or Tuesdays as well. What happened between us was not at all like the days when we had been almost engaged and were going to football games and Saturday night dances.

92

The ritual was that we met—usually after dinner—at the sepulchral marble bench across the street from the Fogg Museum. There, we sat for a few minutes, talking of lofty matters such as current events or organic chemistry while the marble chilled our thighs.

Then, with scarcely a sentence of transition, Cass would stand, and I would follow him to his apartment.

The second time I went there—before it became a habit— he informed me rather harshly as he double locked the door: "We shouldn't lie down when we do this—it isn't right."

So, for some uncomfortable minutes, we grappled side by side. Then, perhaps because the sofa was, after all, only a cot with understuffed pillows wedged against the wall, we found ourselves prone—as though flattened by an unseen hand.

Still, although his knee occasionally nudged between my legs, our hands did not wander. That was the unstated rule Cass had made for us.

Another element in our embraces was music. Cass didn't use music as background for poetry the way Abbott did. Instead, he understood composers, themes and forms, and tried to teach me about them.

That fall, with money earned from a late August baby sitting job my mother had found for me, I bought my first Classical record—Beethoven's "Eroica," Cass's favorite. Disappointingly, it didn't sound the same when I wasn't lying down.

During the last week of summer school when my head was crammed with French grammar and the concerts on the Charles were over, Abbott took me out for dinner two nights running.

On Wednesday, we were at a small French restaurant on the Boston side overlooking the water. On Thursday—Abbott was leaving early Friday to tour England with his mother for three weeks—we went to a luxurious roof garden restaurant in a new apartment house in Cambridge.

The rug there was so thick my heels sank in. Seated before

a white tablecloth that brushed the floor with Abbott ordering wine from a special menu, I wished I were wearing something as striking as the low-cut, full-skirted, pale blue dress Honey had worn when Have took her dancing.

Probably she would have been kind enough to lend it to me—but she had already gone home to Vermont, where her father was a certified public accountant. I never heard the whole story. I merely came back from class one day to find her things were gone. On my bureau, scrawled in the wrong side of a Sociology test in which she'd received a "C," was a pencilled note:

"Can't stay. Don't tell Have."

But if Have was looking for her, he didn't ask me, and later, in a few lines in the back of a Christmas card, she told me she was engaged to someone else.

Anyway, when Abbott climbed to my rooms for the first time after that last dinner, we had the place to ourselves. He had come to help me pack my books, and he was very nice about taking off his jacket and rolling up his sleeves and fitting volumes of the Modern Library series into cartons I'd gotten from the grocery store.

When he had finished, he piled the boxes neatly in the entryway where it would be easy for my mother and brother, who were driving up Saturday to get me, to pick them up. Then standing in the center of the bare study, he kissed me several times in a way that made me think of the way he recited poetry. It didn't seem to be flesh I was encountering as his head blocked the light of the gooseneck lamp on my desk behind him, but words.

Then, as his mouth moved to my neck and the brush-like ends of his hair tickled my chin, the movements of his shoulders seemed rhythmic, even metrical. *"I'm serious."* He addressed my left ear in a way that made my stomach contract despite the opulent meal I'd eaten. Then, breaking away with a look that sent chills up my back, he added: "In the fall, I want you to meet my mother."

That was the last time I saw Abbott until October, and the next afternoon, I went to Cass's apartment for the final time.

He too was leaving, although he was keeping the apartment. He was going home to rural Maine, where his father was a general practitioner. After Labor Day, Barbara was returning from California to spend a week with his family.

Cass was poor—he was one of six children—and the people his father treated often didn't pay. I had skipped lunch, but since we had stopped eating together and going to plays several weeks before, ostensibly as a prelude to our permanent separation, I hesitated to ask him to take me out for a sandwich.

We lay down immediately as usual, but somehow it seemed different in the daylight, even though Cass had drawn the shades. A sun beam from a jagged tear at the top of the blind warmed my forehead, and for some reason, maybe because I was hungry, I was unable to lie quietly in his arms as I had so many times before.

Perhaps because he sensed my restlessness, he pressed painfully against me in a new way. Crushed, I felt as if the marble bench across from the Fogg Museum had been turned upside down and lowered into my frame.

Then, in a voice I didn't know I had, I told him: "Get off me!"

He did. But then, standing there with his back to the sunlight, he lectured me with a violence of which I wouldn't have thought him capable.

I was lying there on my back with my stomach rumbling, and he was shouting at me over the last movement of Beethoven's *Ninth*. He was incoherent. I don't remember most of it, but one of the last things he said was: "You've got a *lot* to learn. You don't know anything!"

And then, surprising myself again, I got up and faced him.

"You don't *either*," I told him. "You don't understand me at all—and furthermore" (it was a *non sequitur*) "I'm not going back to the volunteers!"

But what did he care? And besides, why explain?

Without even stopping at the mirror to comb my hair, I left him in the middle of "Freude, Freude."

"The *reason* you don't understand me," I threw back as I slammed the door, "is that you're too damned smart."

In the fall, I had been back at Wellesley several weeks before Abbott called. "My mother developed severe dyspepsia in England," he informed me in sepulchral tones. "She was in the hospital in Leeds for three days and then, after I got her back to London, she could barely leave the room."

"I was a week late starting classes," he continued, "and now I have mountains of work to make up, but—" his voice dropped to the rasping tone he used when reciting poetry, "I've told her *all* about you."

Ridiculously for a moment, I took that to mean he had found out about me and Cass and, at the same time, discovered I'd never gone back to Youth Volunteers even though I'd been elected corresponding secretary for the coming academic year. Then, swallowing, I managed to answer: "That was good of you."

"Yes, and even though she isn't quite up to snuff, she wants to meet you Saturday. I'll pick you up at eight. A friend of hers is coming by, and we'll all play bridge."

It was Wednesday, and girls I knew who were popular always had weekend plans by Tuesday at the latest, usually, if the phones weren't too busy, by Monday night. But what was the point of standing on ceremony when I hadn't even had a letter from Cass—and there wouldn't even be a mixer dance at Wellesley until early November?

Besides, Abbott's mother called him during the middle of the conversation. He had to go and fill a prescription for her. The drug store would be closing.

On Thursday afternoon, when I should have been in the library studying for a Friday quiz in a course called "Intellectual and Cultural History of the Western World," I went shopping. The dress I chose—a long sleeved green wool that cost almost two months allowance even on sale—made me look older than I was, I decided. It had small, conservative-looking buttons with loops all the way up the front and was—I wondered if Abbott would notice—almost the same color as the leather portfolio of poems he'd given me.

Thursday I had to stay up very late studying the Dark Ages. Friday morning, I muddled through the quiz, struggling right up until the bell rang to compose a commentary on a quote from Boethius that said: "It is the nature of all bodily pleasure to punish those who enjoy it."

Then, after lunch, I went to the library and worked right through dinner. I was sleepy—but determined. I was preparing a surprise for Abbott—for the ride back, after I met his mother.

On Saturday, Abbott was punctual, but he looked different. Perhaps it was his dark suit and tie that made me wonder whether the dress I had chosen was formal enough. (Should I have picked something low-cut and full skirted, perhaps in taffeta?)

Also, he had had a haircut. He had lost the unruly summer school brush that rose from his crown. His hair was neatly parted and licked down—which made it look darker. Instead of resembling an unkempt but engaging Mercury, he merely looked like a businessman, a banker—or anybody else at all.

During the drive to Beacon Hill, he told me about the Lake District and Stonehenge, which they had visited when his mother was well enough to travel.

His house, predictably I suppose, was large and well furnished. His mother, in spite of having been sick, was a big, vigorous woman who might have been described as strapping if she hadn't been so impeccably dressed in a Navy blue suit adorned with a diamond cluster that was meant to look like a flower but instead struck me as a warning beacon.

I was too dressed up after all. Her friend, a woman her own age whom she referred to as "Martha dear," was wearing a suit of similar description except that it was pale olive—a color that made my green dress look garish. The rhinestone buttons that had drawn me to my dress in the beginning were crudely crafted, I realized. The peplum below the waist and the ruffles at the cuffs were fussy—almost cheap looking.

As we played bridge—luckily Abbott held most of the cards and I was dummy a lot—his mother plied me with questions. First the standard ones—where was I from and what courses was I taking. Then, other ones such as what had my father done and would my brother be sent away to a private school.

If I'd been clever, I would have seen where the questions were leading, but in my mind the evening was only a tiresomely formal prelude to *afterwards*, when, hopefully Abbott would take off his tie, ruffle his hair so that it looked the way it had in the summer, and recite Eliot or his own quartets in the way I wanted to hear for the rest of my life. Then, when he was finally exhausted, breathless, I would present him with my surprise.

"And your mother," Abbott's mother asked as I was in the midst of playing the one good hand I held all evening, "What does she do to amuse herself with your father gone?"

"She works as a receptionist in a dentist's office," I told her quickly, trumping the ace I knew she'd been holding, "so that I can stay at Wellesley."

"Oh." As soon as the hand was over, Abbott's mother excused herself to get our tea and cookies, and she didn't ask me anymore questions after that.

Later—I have to admit it was *years* later—I saw the way I should have put things. But then, well, perhaps Cass had been right in saying I didn't know anything. My virginity extended beyond the physical to other things that counted.

If I had "happened" to mention that my father had been Phi

Beta Kappa at Cornell and that his brother was a senior (hence affluent) partner in a well-known New York law firm, the picture would have been different. Also, I could have alluded to the remote possibility that my brother would attend Andover without mentioning that he would need a scholarship, and I could have painted my mother's job as a lighthearted diversion—"something she just <u>had</u> to try because she was so lonely at home." Thus, I might have given a marginally acceptable account of myself without actually lying.

But then, I hadn't learned that the only thing which counted with the rich was being rich. It was all a matter of money. Yet, years later, when I began to write myself, I still remembered the way Abbott had recited poetry.

That night, when the game broke up before we'd finished the second rubber, I was in for a disappointment. "Aunt Martha," as Abbott called her even though she wasn't a relative, lived in Wellesley Hills. Of course, we were to drive her home.

That meant—after Abbott had escorted her to the door and returned to the car—that there was only a little way left. Not far enough for Abbott to get going on poetry.

Anyway, for reasons I didn't fathom then, he was very reserved for the rest of the drive. At the door of my dormitory, without even making a pretense of kissing me, he very formally wished me a successful year at college, adding that he hoped I would go on to and read Pound.

Without getting the gist of it beyond being disappointed that we hadn't gotten to the point of poetry, I was determined not to let my surprise go to waste.

So there, without any preface—just standing on the grass in front of all the lighted dormitory windows with drawn curtains—I recited "Complainte de l'oubli des mortes" all the way through in French from memory. Pretty good French at that— I'd gotten my grade in the mail from Harvard the week before, and it was an "A."

"Importun
Vent qui rage!
Les défunts?
Ça voyage."

As I finished the last stanza, I felt in myself the intensity I'd sensed in the summer in him. I was trembling, expectant.

But, retreating a little toward the privet hedge that screened the parking lot, he only stared at me. At last, after an uncomfortable pause, he admitted: "I never took French, you know. My family—my mother—thought Latin and German counted more."

"Yes—" I was still caught up in the lines, which I had come to admire even more as I spoke them, "—but it's *Laforgue*, you know, the one that Eliot was so—"

"Yes," he offered. "I know Matthiessen said he was an important influence, but I've never—"

His shoes grated on the gravel, he was backing down the path. The amazing thought struck me that I might have listened more closely to Matthiessen than Abbott had—and done more of the assigned readings.

But before I could begin to absorb what this might mean, he favored me with a final, almost lackadaisical, wave—and was gone. I heard his footsteps on the macadam, and then, nothing.

A line from Eliot—I didn't know which poem—crossed my mind. It was: "They all go into the dark."

That winter, when time came for the Junior Prom, someone had to get me a blind date. Not only had I never heard from either Abbott or Cass, I'd also failed to meet anyone at the November mixer.

When I went home for Christmas, I read in *The New York Times* of Cass's engagement to Barbara. She was a New York debutante—he hadn't told me that. The couple would be married in June and live in Boston.

A Rough Ride

Is it possible that a story can have a *color*? If so, this re-membrance is Burnt Sienna, a harsh, excremental hue I've never liked. Naples Yellow, not so far away on the color chart, has a mellow, even-aristocratic, after-sunset glow, but Burnt Sienna is as raw and unexpected as an inexplicable rust stain on a white collar or a blotch of long-dried blood on a crackled tile in an old-fashioned bathroom. Burnt Sienna evokes the wrench-ing moment of nausea preceded by dizziness, the not-to-be-discounted premonition of misfortune, and finally, the damp, moist color of the earth—perhaps lightly mingled with sand—piled beside an open grave.

But what does Burnt Sienna, or for that matter, the sunniest Cadmium Yellow on the palette, have to do with my discovery of Julianna and Theodore—not as they appeared when pic-tured in glossy magazines about country life or artistic achieve-ment—but as they were? It was all happenstance—a contriv-ance of fortune objectified and thus made memorable—like a muddy handprint on a pale wall or a rosebud crushed, inad-vertently, beneath a heavy heel.

My parents, who had surely been as attractive as the Livingstons seemed to me at first, were a decade and a half dead in a yachting accident. I was 19 and alone in New York "taking courses" which, point of fact, I seldom attended. Julie and Teddy, as they wanted me to call them even though she was well into her forties and he, certainly fifty, had been friends—"dear friends" they often hastened to say, of my late parents. Fortuitously, I had met them because we were sitting on the same bench in Gramercy Square Park.

I had access to the private, always-locked enclave because I was living in an economical (most of my parents' assets had washed away in the stock market shortly after the sinking) women's residence on the south side of the square. They had access because they had "always" had a penthouse in one of

101

the tall, elegant, north side apartment buildings that I sometimes peered up at from the single window of my narrow, white-
walled chamber.

On a warm morning in October, we happened to be sharing,
as I said, the same bench—I on one end, Julianna on the other.
I had a book, a large one that took two hands to hold. She had
a little green leather-covered sketchbook and a pencil. Between
us sat Teddy, who was wearing a dapper grey suit and a striped
tie. He was reading *The New Yorker* magazine. When an in-
sert, possibly a subscription coupon, fell to the ground, I picked
it up for him.

He thanked me. He introduced himself, Julianna nodded a
bit distantly. He fell to talking to me about my book, an anthol-
ogy, and after we had been discussing the selections for a few
minutes, I told him my first name.

"La-vin-i-a," he mused, turning over the syllables like a loz-
enge on his tongue. "We knew a Lavinia. Lavinia—"

"Macmoines," Julianna cut in.

I stared at her, noticing the way the sun coming through the
trees glinted on her necklace of sea blue beads—possibly aqua-
marines. "That was my mother's name."

I saw a shadow—perhaps it was only the movement of high
boughs swayed by the breeze—cross her face. Then there were
smiles, exclamations; I found myself shaking hands with both
of them at once.

"But," Julianna was saying, "you must have been just a baby
when—"

"I was four—"

Teddy was shaking his head sympathetically, "—that they
should take the boat out alone in the face of a storm—"

"—a *hurricane*," Julianna added.

"It seemed so *feckless*," Teddy went on, "but where have
you been all these years, dear, how did you manage to—?"

Before I could even begin the saga of how I had been spir-
ited upstate from the pre-kindergarten of an upper East Side

school to the ageing, turn-of-the-century Utica mansion of a great aunt of my mother's, my only relative except for a second cousins of my father's who lived in Michigan, Teddy interrupted. "The luncheon's at twelve—"

"Oh yes," Julianna explained, "he'll be signing his new book."

Only then, belatedly, did I realize Teddy was *the* Theodore Ulysses Livingston, author of architectural books that were usually about New York State. His big volume on the Victorian style in the Mohawk Valley had long reposed on Aunt Anna's parlor table beneath her Tiffany reading lamp. It was the only one that contained the precious photograph of the once-grand block where she had lived all her life *before* the beautiful old house on the corner had been torn down for a filling station.

Now Aunt Anna's stroke, the day after my graduation from high school, had led to the storing of her books and all her furniture—things she had apparently intended to leave to me. Soon after had come the suspiciously quick sale of her house to downtown developers by lawyers whom I would not be able to deal with until I was 21, and perhaps not even then, unless—contrary to her doctors' predictions—she could be roused from her coma.

The Livingstons were leaving. I rose to say good-bye. Julianna (he was Teddy to me from the first, but I never felt comfortable calling her Julie) snapped her sketchbook shut. I caught no more than a glimpse of her lightly-pencilled drawing of what seemed to be a bushy, soft-needled pine tree.

Predictable as the happy endings in the old children's books I had read at Aunt Anna's was the Livingstons' kind insistence on seeing me again. As Teddy tipped his hat, Julianna informed me: "Since we're not going to the country this weekend, dear, we're having a little party. Some old friends of your parents will be there—you must come. We'll introduce you to everyone."

I nodded, noticing as Julianna leaned toward me that although her pale skin appeared thin, perhaps even brittle, she had few wrinkles. She was old, from my perspective, but not so old, I realized, that a man—a man her age—could not consider her beautiful. If my mother had lived, I wondered, would she have looked like that?

But what can be postulated from a few fading snapshots? What could have been is nothing; what <u>does</u> happen, even by the flimsiest coincidence, is everything. As I sat down on the bench again, wondering whether to go to my class, which bored me, or simply return my book to the library and browse in the stacks, it seemed to me that the chance meeting with the Livingstons had been inevitable.

I had been in New York since late August, and it was almost November. I had attended classes, visited museums and libraries, and yes, fallen in love with Roland, a journalist now on assignment abroad. *Something* else had to happen, didn't it?

Then, deciding to write another letter to Roland in Africa, although I had not heard from him for several weeks, I went back to my room. Later, it seemed to me that morning had been destined—just as inexorably as the morning long before when Aunt Anna had appeared at the class Halloween party unannounced because "Mommy and Daddy had gone away for a long time"—to reshape my life.

My choices of what to wear to the Livingston's party on Friday were not numerous. There was the white, plain well-cut dress that Aunt Anna had helped me pick for my high school graduation ceremonies. That was definitely out of season, so my only other choice was the dark blue wool she had given me the previous Christmas. I hadn't liked it much at the time: it was drab and far more formal that the clothes anyone I knew in school would wear, but when she presented it to me with palsied hands on what turned out to be our last Christmas in the high-ceilinged old front parlor, all I could do was thank her. I had long before accepted the fact that I—an orphan living with a far-from-wealthy old woman in an antiquated mansion in what had become the wrong part of town—could not "keep up" with the classmates I liked best and would have wished to emulate.

I put on the blue dress, which had long sleeves and ribbed stitching radiating our from a high neckline, when I returned to my solitary room Friday afternoon from a class in which I had not been paying attention. The dress, visible only to the waist in the speckled mirror above the white wooden bureau enlivened by Roland's picture and the small pile of his letters, struck me as severe, even dreary—but what choice did I have?

Aunt Anna had always talked, grandly, of sending me to one of the prominent colleges in New England. I had applied—and been accepted. Then, in July, after an afternoon spent with the lawyers discussing "back taxes, old debts and medical obligation," I had withdrawn. There would be a monthly check, it had been explained to me. It would—if that was what I wanted—be enough for "living simply in New York and taking a course or two." It would not be enough for large bi-annual tuition payments "until the estate was settled"—and perhaps never. So, even on the occasion of what I believed would be my reentry into my parents' world, I could not afford to rush out and buy something new.

After riding to the penthouse in the company of a grey-uniformed elevator operator, the first thing that struck me at the Livingston's party was the sense of being an inconspicuous ultramarine shadow in a great splash of color. It was a large, sumptuous, vividly decorated apartment, and, since it was a warm evening, there were guests on the broad, south-facing terrace with its potted shrubs. Guests also filled the living room with its brightly patterned, overstuffed couches and its walls crowded with paintings, the dining room with its long, antique table and its scenic wall paper, and the library with its leather chairs and rows of books, some of which had been written by Teddy himself.

At first, awkward and uncertain, I despaired that I would even be noticed by the self-assured men and beautifully-turned-out women who, it seemed to me, must all be as brilliant and knowledgeable as the Livingstons, or perhaps—the thought struck me—as my parents had been. Pausing in a corner while other guests brushed past me because I did not see either Teddy or Julianna, I felt it was almost possible that I would here again encounter those shades who were merely unsatisfactory and tantalizingly incomplete memories—smell my mother's faintly-remembered perfume, feel the warm clasp of my father's hand.

Eventually, the hand that possessed me was not my father's, of course, it was Teddy's. Taking me firmly by the elbow, he steered me into the center of the living room overlooking the terrace and began to introduce me to people whose names I would never remember as "the daughter of my dear dead friend John Macmoines."

Aunt Anna had told me that my father had been a well-known editor at a publishing house that after his death merged with another company. But what did that mean in Utica, a city of merchants, bankers and lawyers? It was the maiden name of my mother, who at least had grown up there, which counted if anything did. But even her name, which was Aunt Anna's, and also, the name of the downtown square that memorialized my mother's grandfather, the founder of a newspaper, were nothing but historic curiosities in a place where others, albeit relative new-comers, had long since become richer and more powerful.

In New York, at least, I was more than an isolated orphan subsisting on an ancient relative's kindness. Instead, at least in these circles, I had status as one presumed to have inherited certain talents. I was asked, immediately and repeatedly, if I planned "to go into publishing" or if I "wanted to write." The assumption, when I knew I might never even graduate from college, that such aims were even remotely within my reach was troubling but exciting.

I knew I couldn't tell them I had dreamed of nothing more than marrying Roland, possibly in the spring, and accompanying him on future trips, wherever he went. So, long before the end of the evening, I found myself smiling in a way that suggested affirmation when asked one of those questions—or even nodding.

Even my blue ink blot dress, which stood out so starkly against the flowered taffetas and the tailored satins the other women were wearing, was something of an asset. The dress, as well as my long hair, an oddity in the assembly of well-coiffed matrons, set me apart. The other thing that distinguished me—and I began to see that it was more powerful than I had suspected—was my youth.

There were men, men older than Roland but too young to remember my father, who wanted to talk to me. Their hands clasped and unclasped my wrists, their fingers stroked my hair, entwined themselves in my unkempt curls. None was as attractive as Roland, certainly, but there was one who—

His name was Arthur, and he seemed to know Julianna and Teddy very well. He was perhaps forty, perhaps younger. He, like my father, was an editor. He had, in fact, edited Teddy's new volume, a study of Carpenter Gothic houses in New York State. The book, he told me, was "a significant contribution, but not a money-earner."

"Does Julianna write books too?" I asked.

He looked at me. "Julie's a painter—I thought you knew."

"I knew that she sketched—" Since he knew the Livingstons so well, I hesitated to admit my acquaintance was so brief that I scarcely knew them at all.

"She painted almost everything in this room—"

"Oh—" Squinting—I was nearsighted, but I hadn't worn my glasses—I peered self-consciously at the large, pale-toned canvases hanging over the mantelpiece, above the side tables, and in the corner behind a grand piano artfully half-covered by a tasseled shawl. The subjects, as far as I could make out, were such things as flowers immersed in flowing water, street puddles gleaming with the reflections of glowing lights, and intricately patterned fabrics on which leaves, branches and bric-a-brac were scattered in artistic disorder.

I had wandered through New York museums, but the paintings I knew best were the old- fashioned, gilt-framed oils I had grown up with in Aunt Anna's parlors. The largest was a view of a stag poised against an Adirondack mountain backdrop; the smallest was a delicate depiction of a country couple in a one horse carriage. The most valuable was a grand rendering, said to have been purchased at the Salon in Paris, of a ship in full sail.

I knew enough to know that Julianna's works were not old fashioned—but not abstract and modern either. "She's talented," I began hesitantly.

"Very," Arthur affirmed. "She had a show in an uptown gallery last spring, but it didn't make much of a splash. She's good, but these days, youth is everything. She should have done more—*sooner*. She *could* have, since they've never had children. She ought to have gotten going years ago, but somehow—" Arthur paused, reached for an engraved silver box on the coffee table, offered me a cigarette, and when I declined, lit his own.

"It's vital," Arthur went on, "to *go*—for it at the beginning." He paused, his face came closer to mine, peering down. "Someone like *you*, with a name that's not unknown, *you* could write something, you could—"

The smoke he was exhaling filled my nose, burning unpleasantly. The idea that I could—or should—write *anything* was becoming disagreeable, overwhelming. What could I—only a few months out of the honors program of an upstate school—have to say?

I drew back, coughed. "I *couldn't*—"

108

I remembered that on one of Aunt Anna's shelves there was a book of poems printed on pale blue, handmade paper. It had been written by my mother before I was born. I'd read it, but not for a long time, and all I could truthfully recall was one about "My Heart's Flight" in which "Thee" and Thou" were used many times. I was not, I decided, going to tell Arthur about *that*.

Perhaps sensing my discomfiture, Arthur became less pressing. "Well, perhaps you are a bit young," he admitted, "but don't wait forever. You're beautiful, you know, and that always helps." He paused, snuffed out his cigarette in a cloisonné ash tray. "Julie, in her own way, has everything, except perhaps that she married Teddy too young—"

"Is that so bad?" I broke in. I had hopes that Roland and I would become engaged when he came back for Christmas.

"Not necessarily," he told me, "but as I'm sure you've heard, he's given her a very rough ride—"

For a moment, I pictured Julianna mounted on a brown, wildly plunging horse. Her face was pale, her skirts forced to upper thighs. "You mean—"

There was no opportunity for Arthur to explain. Julianna had made her way through the crowd, now thinning as it was long after sunset, to take his hand. Turning, he planted a kiss on her cheek.

"I was just telling little Lavinia," he began, leaving me to wonder how well he knew Juliana, "what an excellent painter you are, dearest."

Smiling, Julianna stretched out her free hand for my hand. "And I have come to tell Lavinia that we're *determined* to see her again. Don't listen to a thing Arthur tells you," she added quickly, "he's naughty and full of flatteries." Then, turning to face me, she declared: "Teddy and I are going to the country next weekend. It's up the Hudson—Arthur has a house there too. We want to take you with us. Can you do it?"

I had no idea where "up the Hudson" might be, but I felt

certain it was not a place like Utica. There was no reason at all I couldn't accept, yet, connected uncomfortably to Arthur by Julianna's hand, I hesitated. Then some guests came to say good-bye, and I was relieved to be disconnected from both of them.

There seemed to be no one else to talk to, so I wandered out on the terrace by myself, staring down across the park at the residence where I was living. From so high up, I saw, the perspective of the square was very different. The park looked small; branches hid my third floor window. What was it like, I wondered, to live at the top, to be known and sought-after as the Livingstons were, and as, I imagined, my parents had been?

If my parents had lived, I mused, I would surely be attending college, and perhaps, even boldly dreaming of doing something significant afterwards. Then, in a potted, late-blooming rosebush dimly illuminated by the lights inside, I saw something was moving on the petals of a half-opened bud whose color was lost in shadows. Peering down, I saw it was a beetle. Although it was too dark to be sure, I concluded it was the red-brown kind that ate from within, riddling living petals so they browned before blooming, loosened in the barest breeze, dropped down to dust.

Then, unexpectedly, a fatherly arm encircled my waist. It was Teddy. "Of what, little girl," he asked jovially, "are you dreaming?"

Briefly, I pictured that Roland had returned to take me in his arms. I didn't want to tell Teddy that, so I said: "Of something, I suppose, that I can't remember."

He looked at me. "We all have those dreams, don't we?" He dropped his arm and we wandered, as if by mutual consent, to lean on the brick parapet, staring south.

"I almost fell in love with your mother once," he told me. "She was very beautiful—" He had been drinking, I realized, not too much, perhaps, but enough so that I smelled it.

"I can't helping wishing they hadn't—" I confided.

"Of course." There was a pause. "Sometimes, I wonder if dreaming of things that can't be isn't better. Often, when you get what you want—" His voice trailed off.

I couldn't think of an answer, so we just stood there, facing the greyish brown sky pinkened by all the lights. Eventually, Julianna came and stood beside me. A look passed between the Livingstons over my head, but I could not guess it's meaning.

"She's coming with us next weekend," Teddy told Juliana.

"Of course she is," Julianna affirmed. Their arms twined over my shoulders, meeting behind my back as I stood silent between them. I had not said I would come, but like an obedient child, I knew I would do what they wanted.

It was arranged that Teddy and Julianna would pick me up the next Friday afternoon for the drive up the Hudson. Their "country place." they told me, had a view of the river. Perhaps because I had skipped class again and read all day in the library, I was tired. I dozed almost from the time I arranged myself in the back seat of their convertible with my small bag until, after a brief stop for something to eat, we arrived about ten at their big old wooden house that was somewhat outside of a small town and perched on a grassy hillock among trees.

If the Hudson was nearby, I couldn't see it, but from the tracks that ran along the river, I heard the noise of a train. Shown to my little back room, I hung my blue dress in the closet. Then I got into the narrow, white iron bed over which hung a photograph of a little girl, possibly Julianna, with a dog. The weather had changed, the sheets were cold, but after pulling up the stitched, flowered quilt, I fell asleep immediately.

There, facing a little gable with a casement window, I slept for a long time and dreamed prodigiously. In my dreams, a day lengthened interminably until it seemed to encompass my entire life.

First, I was a child, living with my parents in an apartment that seemed much like Julianna's and Teddy's. Then, with no apparent transition, I was grown up and married to Roland, but we were not living in his small but cozy west Greenwich Village apartment where he had promised we would spend Christmas and have a fire in the fireplace. Instead, we were living upstate in Utica with Aunt Anna who, though at first dying, recovered and grew younger while I aged rapidly. As I awakened, finally, to the smell of bacon and coffee, I was already grey and tired and a widow, but Aunt Anna, a charming child with ringlets, was my responsibility and my joy.

It took a long time for me to wake up that morning, even though my watch told me it was after ten. Clearly, the Livingstons had been too kind to call me, even though they must have eaten breakfast much earlier. There was a note waiting for me on the kitchen table beside a platter of bacon, and my place was set with pretty china ringed with pink rosebuds. I was to take, the note said, whatever I wanted. They had gone shopping.

After I had eaten, washed my dishes and wiped the table carefully—I was eager to be considered a good guest—I began to explore the house, which I had scarcely seen the night before.

The house was old, a half century older than Aunt Anna's, but unlike hers, it was a recently purchased reconstruction—rather than an inherited continuation—of the past. I had glanced at Teddy's new book about Carpenter Gothic houses at the party, and I knew places like this were countrified, pattern-book versions of the High Gothic fashion glorified in churches and other public buildings. Depending more on rustic saws and rural chisels than on affluence or inspiration, the dust jacket had declared, such relatively humble rural retreats bespoke a romantic reaction to the grand, many-columned, Greek Revival mansions.

The Livingston's front room, I saw, was freshly painted in delicate earth tones. There was a restored chandelier that illuminated highly polished examples of side pieces with Gothic curliques. Everything from the draperies to the rugs to the pillows on the antique sofa reupholstered in velvet—probably at great expense—suggested a concerted striving, probably by a decorator, for a "period" look.

Just down the hall in which immaculately fresh wallpaper pictured Gothic ruins alternating with ivy-entwined gazebos, was the long, book-lined room that had to be Teddy's study. There, lunettes alternated with high-arched shelves, and, at the far end where the massive desk stood, the casements of the bowed out window were set with diamonds of lavender, amber, garnet and viridian-colored glass that were so clear, so uncracked, I suspected many were modern replacements. The study, apart from the pantry and adjoining dining room, a back vestibule and a lavatory, completed the public part of a house even I knew was "smart" in a way Aunt Anna's shabby mansion—now soon to be demolished—never could have been.

I had thought of exploring the grounds, which sloped down to a grove of trees that only partially obscured the railroad tracks, and beyond them, the river, but a fine rain was beginning. Deciding to get a book from my suitcase, I made my way upstairs. About to go down the hall to my room, I instead turned guiltily in the other direction, where two doors stood open. In the large room on the right, obviously the master, there was a large, unmade bed on which the chintz cover thrown carelessly over the footboard matched the ruffled, half-open curtains at the two front windows. Cast to the floor on a pink carpet beside the bed was a woman's white silk nightgown.

Then, turning to peer into the second room, which opened a little further toward the window seat at the end of the hall, I saw it contained twin beds, one of which had been slept in. At the foot of that bed, also unmade, was a nice-looking pair of short-topped tan leather boots that had to be Teddy's.

Just then, I heard dance music coming from the radio in the kitchen below my room. Quickly smoothing my hair, I made

113

the bed. Then, carrying my book under my arm, I went downstairs to find the Livingstons fixing lunch.

How attractive and compatible they seemed together. While she tossed the salad, he set the table in the dining room with pretty little French luncheon plates. As we ate, the music pealed forth merrily, the rain stopped, and the sun streamed in through the casements facing the Hudson, illuminating the fall flowers Julianna had arranged for a centerpiece and the generous carafe of red wine. As she cleared the table, Teddy playfully tied an apron around her waist and planted an affectionate kiss on her cheek.

Although what I wanted most was to have them tell me about my parents, it was I—under the influence of their wine, their conviviality, who did most of the talking. Teddy was interested in Aunt Anna's house and what it had contained. Julianna, who had never been to Utica, wanted to know what paintings hung in the museum.

As we lingered over small cups of strong coffee that Teddy had bought at "a special little place in New York," I almost forgot the separate bedrooms. Perhaps he snored or she was an insomniac. Finally, I became confident enough in their union to ask: "My parents—you knew them very well—what were they like? Were they happy?"

There was the smallest pause, and almost at the same moment, the tango that was playing on the radio ended. Then, both of the Livingstons began to answer my questions at once.

"The were blissfully happy, I'm sure," Teddy told me. "Your mother was a captivating woman, and your father, although he may have been careless about money and unwise in taking their boat out when bad weather had been predicted, was a superb editor. The men who have taken his place—you met Arthur— are perfectly good fellows, but they see books—even the kind I write—as commercial productions. To your father a book— a really *good* book—was a work of art."

While Teddy went on about books, his own in particular,

Julianna, leaning toward me, added quietly: "Of course they were happy, don't you see dear, they had *you*."

I remembered the little photograph over the bed in my room. Nearby was an ornate, old-fashioned, child-sized rocker. It had clearly been collected, like everything else, to "go" with the house, but was there another meaning—a forlorn, reluctantly abandoned hope?

Finally Teddy, who was far from concise when it came to detailing his own projects, turned the conversation to the article on 19th century octagonal houses he was writing for a prominent magazine. Eventually, he announced that, "It's time to do some work."

As he retreated to his study, I assumed, for the rest of the afternoon, Julianna declared she wanted to "show off her studio." So, taking me by the hand, she led me up a twisting back stair in a closet behind the kitchen to a third floor I had not known existed. There, in the slanting light of gables, and, at the far end, a high lancet, stood an easel flanked by several tables containing tubes of paint and brushes. Beyond, close to one of the gables under which canvases of varying sizes were stacked side by side, was an odd, rose red plush lounge that had claw feet and rose up in a portly, overstuffed fashion, at one end of which were piled pillows with tasseled edges and, falling unevenly to the floor in a whirlpool of shimmering fabric, a multi-colored throw that looked exotic, possibly Oriental.

"This is my den," Julianna told me with a little tinkling laugh. "There isn't room enough in New York, so I'm a Sunday painter, and Saturdays too. In summer though, we're here most of the time."

The place struck me as a "quotation" from her paintings at the apartment. The colors of the studio were soft and shadowy, melting into each other like warm wax.

"Would you like to sketch, dear?" Julianna asked. "I could give you paper and pastels—or oils if you'd like them. There's a lovely view of the river if you sit at the back window."

I shook my head. "I have no talent. Aunt Anna saw to it that I had art lessons—and piano lessons too. I enjoyed using the colors, hearing their names, but even my teachers admitted that—"

"Oh well—" she hesitated. "You can do as you please then—read your book, take a walk. We're all going to a party together tonight that friends are giving, there'll be some young people there, I'm quite sure—so you'll have a good time."

"I'm used to older people," I told her, "—growing up with Aunt Anna." I didn't dare add that although there were some women in Utica who remembered my mother as a girl, I had never met any of her contemporaries who had known her *later*, after I was born.

"I suppose that's natural," Julianna mused, perhaps thinking of something else. Then, going to the gathering of canvases under the gable, she selected a portrait-sized one and brought it back to the easel. "It must have been lonely, growing up away from people you might have known if your parents hadn't—"

"It was."

Julianna was no taller than I, but she came and put her hands on my shoulders as if I were still a child. "Come and sit down," she said, leading me toward the rose-colored couch. "You'd like to know everything I remember about your mother, wouldn't you?"

Close to tears, I could only nod.

"I'll tell you what I can, child—though it isn't much. I was young then myself, and when you're young you're careless because you think youth, love, and everything else that seems so easy in the beginning will last forever." She sighed, then asked: "While we talk, would it bother you if I did your portrait?"

I shook my head. "Of course not."

"You can lean back, rest against the pillows, even go to sleep.

Even if you move a little now and then, I can still get the likeness." Julianna paused, went to a little shelf I hadn't noticed under one of the gables. She came back to me carrying a carafe that looked Turkish, perhaps Egyptian. It was glass but encased, even to the stopper, in open-work bands of grass. Beside it, there were two little matching goblets. "This isn't good sherry," she told me. "It's the best.'

I was not particularly used to drinking, and the wine I had had at lunch had made me light-headed and sleepy. Still, I let her fill my glass. After she had filled hers, we clicked them together.

"To your mother—"

"To my mother—"

"You must take off that sweater, dear," she told me. "It's terribly warm up here. In an old house like this, heat rises." Her hands were insistent. I had nothing on underneath but a little white undershirt, but dreamily, like a child being put to bed, I followed her instructions. After she had helped me pull the sweater off over my head, her hands lingered on the curve of my arms, her nails raked my palms.

I believe she went back to her easel after that, but afterwards, I was never quite sure. I do remember her voice—hushed, as though beginning a fairy tale. "As you know, your mother was very beautiful. Teddy met her even before he met me, because your father was his editor. When I first knew your mother, I was a little bit envious. I was a painter, and people like Teddy encouraged me, but your mother didn't need to do anything to be admired. People were drawn to her, loved her, men, of course, in particular...."

There was more to the story, but I was so terribly, terribly sleepy. I opened my eyes once or twice and saw she was at her easel, working, but I could not see the canvas. Soon, I was seduced by sleep.

Later, in the window of a gallery on Madison avenue where there was a group show, I saw a little portrait in the window

117

done in Julianna's pale, characteristic colors. It was of a young girl, nude to the waist, sleeping on a silken throw I thought I recognized. The hair was a different color, but the face, I was convinced, was mine. There was no way to be sure though, because I had no clear memory of anything that happened afterwards until somehow, wearing my blue dress, I was sitting in the kitchen downstairs with the Livingstons drinking black coffee.

They took me to the party shortly after, and I was careful to drink nothing but Coke. The only person I knew there was Arthur, who chatted with me at first. Then Julianna appeared.

"Arthur's very dangerous," she told me in a way that might—or might not have meant just the opposite. "I must take him away from you," she added with a sweet little smile, bearing him off with her hand nestled on his arm.

Alone for a minute—Teddy was in the opposite corner of the room engaged in an intense conversation with the hostess, a tall blonde—I wondered why Arthur hadn't married. Did it suggest he cared little for women, or instead, that he and Julianna might—?

Finally, the son of the hostess came and talked to me. He was home for the weekend from college where I'd been accepted. I couldn't resist telling him I'd almost gone there, but after that I weakened, lied. "I couldn't come because of my aunt's illness," I told him. "I may enter in January, or if not, next September."

He believed me, gave me his campus phone number. "Call me when you get there," he told me as if he really meant it.

"Yes," I told him, "I definitely will."

The next morning at breakfast, I learned that Julianna, who was a Catholic, would be going to church while Teddy, who jovially described himself as "an irreligious old reprobate," wouldn't. Teddy had "just finished his article" and was "eager," he said, "to show me some books my father had edited."

Julianna had come to breakfast in a long, pink wool robe with an appliquéd satin monogram over the breast pocket. When she returned to the dining room dressed for church, she was wearing a fitted black coat. Somehow, the dark color made her look older. Although her hair was cut in a youthful way—a long bob with straight bangs that covered most of her forehead, the color—an off-brown with undertones of umber—did not look quite convincing in the grey light of a cloudy, early November morning. At the same time, her ivory-colored skin, which I had admired for its lack of wrinkles, had a thin, papery texture that made her oval face look fragile as fine china. She looked, I saw, a little like a rouged and powdered doll.

After she had gone—she had told us she would be stopping to visit an ancient cousin in a nursing home after church—I dutifully began to clear the table. I was planning to wash the dishes until Teddy begged: "Don't bother—I'll take care of everything later. *Come*—there's so much I want to show you."

I had stopped to crumb the table, gather the dishes in the sink, then, before I could entirely dry my hands, Teddy drew me into the living room, explaining as he went.

"—so you see," he told me, "a Carpenter Gothic house like this was meant to be restful, relaxing, natural. The earth tones, the pointed windows meant to suggest that meeting of branches against the sky, the curliques cut with the then-newly-invented scroll saw and intended to suggest the forms of plants and flowers are all part of the ambiance. We had to do an *immense* amount of work after we bought this place ten years ago, but now—don't you think it's homey?"

I nodded, wondering if I could ever feel at home in such a perfect reconstruction, a place, I felt, that was more artifice than art. Then, as he drew me on toward the library, I lost track of what he was telling me. I was interested in old-fashioned architecture, but not *that* interested. Instead, I became more aware than I had been before of his face.

His head was well-modeled, and almost conventionally

119

handsome. This was offset, slightly, by his thick, steel-rimmed glasses and by his mouth, which was thin-lipped, but somehow gave the impression of being crowded with teeth. Those teeth—some obviously the products of expensive dentistry—included incisors rimmed with gold and molars, quite possibly made of porcelain, that did not quite match the colors of those adjoining.

As Teddy opened the door of the library with what I knew was meant to be an ingratiating smile and told me: "This is my lair," I saw that his mouth seemed to be unusually full of saliva rising from beneath his small, pink tongue.

Once we were in the study that seemed a bit overheated, he shut the heavy door behind us. Then, motioning me to sit on a brown, leather-covered couch beside the fireplace, he began to remove books from the shelves, piling them on the little table that faced us. Then he came and sat beside me, perhaps a little too close.

"This," he began quickly, "was my first book—edited by your father."

"Oh—" I took up a thin volume with a faded dust jacket. It was about early church steeples in New England, and there were black and white photographs, although not many of them, of white wooded examples pointing upward against the cloudless skies.

"Your father was very perceptive," Teddy's well-manicured hand brushed mine as he turned a page. "He published my steeple monograph—one of the first on the subject—but he saw, I think it is fair to say, *intuited*, that my true interest lay in later periods, the 19th century in particular. He encouraged me, shortly before his death, to do this book—" Teddy proffered a thicker, larger volume— "on scenic wallpapers. From that, I turned to Greek Revival mansions, and then to the mid-19th century fashions—perhaps I should say passions—" he smiled, "for the Italianate, the Gothic, and so forth."

"So he didn't actually edit your wallpaper book?" I had the

courage to interrupt.

"No, it was the man they brought in after his death, the one whom Arthur replaced later on, who actually did the editing. But it was your father, I must say, who turned me in the right direction. I was young then, and although he wasn't a great deal older, he—"

"What other books did he edit, besides yours, before he died?"

There was a slight pause. "Well, there were *many*. He started the series on American architects that was carried on after his death by—what was his name—? He was *instrumental* in promoting, in various institutions, the preservation of certain architectural drawings that had been simply cast aside by—"

"I see." What I saw was that, if I wanted a comprehensive picture of what my father really had done, I would have to go to the library and ferret our the facts for myself.

Teddy, perhaps sensing he had disappointed me, rose and went to a corner shelf where there was a pile of his new books. Returning with the top copy, he opened it to a full page color photograph of what I realized was the house we were in. "Without your father," he told me a little too loudly, "I might never have written this book—or purchased this house."

I nodded. What he had told me was generally true, I saw, except for the last, which had the forced, inflated insistence of a eulogy. You could not, I realized, expect people to go on praising and remembering the dead—even to the survivors. If I wanted to know more of my father I would have to ask someone else, and that person might be—no one I would ever meet.

It was sunny outside, I saw through the study's thickly-curtained windows. Abruptly, I wished I could escape the overheated room, run down the sloping hill, cross the tracks and stand beside the river alone—free to forget what had—or hadn't—happened years before, able to merely watch the broad, brown, wordless river as it coursed toward the sea.

Perhaps sensing my restlessness, Teddy offered: "Can I get

you anything?"

"No, thank you—nothing—perhaps a glass of water." I rose as if to accompany him, but he waved me back.

"I'll only be a minute—"

Soon he returned with a glass of what turned out to be mineral water, closing the heavy door again behind him.

Still standing, I drained the glass immediately, while he waited beside me. He had placed himself, I noticed, between me and the big windows with the stained glass panes that tinted the sunlight.

I was about to set the glass on the table beside me, but he took it, holding it between both palms like a cup, and then, turned and abandoned it to a bookshelf.

"Do you know what you are?" he asked me.

I looked at him.

"You are—the sweetest little orphan I've ever met." Without further ado, Teddy gathered me into his arms.

It was an embrace I first wanted to think was fatherly, but that illusion died when his hands slid from my waist to my breasts and he began kissing me on the mouth.

It had been a long time since Roland's departure, and for a moment I savored how good it felt to be held, fondled, desired.

Then, perhaps it was the inadvertent contact with his teeth, which I felt were fragile, artful, perhaps almost entirely artificial, that made me squirm free.

"You're just a baby," he whispered soothingly.

"I'm *not*," I told him softly, purposely drawing my lips back so he could see that my teeth, unlike his, were genuine.

"She won't be back for *several* hours," he replied soothingly. "We could just—"

"We *couldn't*," I told him, "—and besides, *you're* the baby."

The door to his study was heavy, but it opened easily. I made my way up the front stairs, and Teddy did not follow. On the way to my room (I no longer cared if he heard me) I peered into the front bedrooms. As before, I saw, both had been occu-

122

pied.

Once back in my room, I turned the latch, packed , then settled down on the stiff bed to finish my book, which was overdue at the library. My eyes followed black words; my hands turned white pages. My mind, though, pictured confusion of colors. Those shades that seemed to blot out both words and meanings were painfully bright—not politely muted like the tones in Julianna's paintings. A painful red met a sharp blue against the vertigo-yellow. Things I might have said to Teddy— but hadn't, other things I might have told a dear relative or close friend—if such a person had been available, were embodied in the jarring conjunction of those imaginary colors.

At the same time—in the way that you can do one thing while thinking about another—I finished the book. Then, in less time than Teddy had said—certainly no more than an hour, I heard a car in the driveway. Soon, Julianna was tapping on my door, summoning me to a "late pick-up lunch before we leave."

As I put on my shoes, combed my hair, I wondered whether Julianna had returned early from her visit because she had suspected Teddy might—?

At the table—we had soup and sandwiches but no wine— Julianna talked sadly of "Cousin Oscar" who was "probably in no better condition than your poor Aunt," while Teddy sympathized amiably.

Apparently unruffled by what had happened in the study, Teddy insisted, even though I demurred, in presenting me with an unopened round of Camembert that would be "just the thing" when I got back to my "little room" in New York.

If there was any tension between them it was impossible to detect. Instead, as I made my way up the back stairs to collect my belongings, I heard them giggling together companionably, perhaps at some cozy little joke they had not seen fit to tell me.

Riding back to the city afterwards, I tried not to wonder whether the joke was on me. It had already become obvious to me that Julianna had not visited "Cousin Oscar" at all, but had instead gone to see Arthur, or even, a woman. What was much more disturbing was the possibility that she had perhaps told Teddy, lightly and treacherously, of what had—or hadn't—happened in the studio the previous afternoon.

Eventually, because there seemed to be no more to say about my parents—or anything else—we all fell silent, and I merely stared out the steady rain that had begun to blur the windows and at the brown leaves falling, or fallen, from grey roadside trees.

I was riding in the back seat, naturally, and all I should see of Teddy and Juliana was the backs of their heads. Once, I though I saw Teddy observing me in the rear view mirror, but perhaps I was wrong. To all appearances, they could have been a couple driving their daughter somewhere. What clue, after all, would have led anyone passing to guess we were not a family?

As we reached the outskirts of Manhattan, the Livingstons began to talk of the pre-Christmas trip they were planning to Paris, and possibly, "on to Rome." Julianna would of course make sketches, while Teddy would visit many buildings preparatory to a book he was planning on 19th century column capitols.

"We'd love to see you again before we leave, dear," Julianna told me when I could already see the trees of Gramercy Park, "but I'm afraid we'll be so busy in the next week or two—" Her smile, as she half-turned toward the back seat without looking me in the face, was almost convincing.

The car stopped directly in front of the awning of my residence. The street light was out, but amazingly, there was an empty parking space. When Teddy got out to help me with my suitcase, Julianna got out too. "About your parents—" Teddy began almost apologetically, "I wish we could have told you more—"

"Perhaps we didn't know them," Julianna chimed in, "as well as we thought."

What could I say? Voicing perfunctory thanks, I took the bag from Teddy. I was almost sure I would never see them again—unless by accident, in the park—and I didn't want to. Yet, at the end, they were charming. Almost in unison, they each kissed me on one cheek, then stood together just beyond the brightness of the building's lights as I turned away.

When I reached the illuminated, double glass doorway, I looked back, and they waved. Then, I had a terrible urge to call back into the brown waves of shadows that drowned the imposters' faces: "I love you—"

Pausing in the lobby, I removed the unusually fat letter from Africa from my mailbox. I had heard nothing for more than three weeks: obviously, Roland had something important to tell me. As I rode up in the elevator, I considered the possibilities. He would be home earlier than planned. He would not be home for Christmas. He loved me, but he did not want to get married. He wanted to marry me at once. He did not love me. He loved another.

There were other variants, but I was too tired to conjure them. I reached my room and set the letter in front of Roland's picture without opening it. Then, I lay down, I would open the envelope—maybe later in the evening, maybe not until morning.

I had lost enough for the present, I decided, turning on my stomach, I could not afford to lose more. For a moment, I buried my head in the pillow, but then, even though it was early, I got up, undressed, snapped off the light. In bed again, I lay on my back in the dark with my eyes open.

The bed faced the window, and the shade was up. High in a corner of the sky was a half moon seemingly facing the wrong way—its dark side to the left. Then, raising myself up on my elbows, I saw that although the trees had blocked the sight of my window from the Livingstons' terrace, I could see their windows and the water tower on the roof through my topmost panes.

As I stared, the lights up there flicked off. Were they going to bed so early, presumably, not together? There was no way to be sure, and perhaps those were not their windows at all, perhaps I was mistaken. What did I know of them, my drowned parents, myself?

I had lost my parents—and had been found by Aunt Anna. Then, as I was about to lose her, I had found Roland. After losing him, perhaps only temporarily, I had come across the Livingstons. Now....

My thoughts blurred. If I did marry Roland would he give me a rough ride—or I him? There was no way to foreguess because, knowing so little of my parents, it was hard to predict myself. All I had of them was—*me*.

Growing very sleepy, I got up and drew the shade. The moonlight filtered in through the thin material; my pillow was a pale rectangle—and so was the letter on the bureau. Between such points of reference there were only shadows—red-brown uncertainties that seemed to be the color I liked least, Burnt Sienna.

Cherry Pie

Maybe it had to end at a locked door I wouldn't unlock. Maybe it didn't. When a man like that wants a girl like me, it can't be a boxes of candy courtship, can it? Sweet temptation almost has to turn to sour apples—or cherries, as the case may be.

I was crossing the North Atlantic in November on an ancient Italian liner. The age of transatlantic passenger crossings was over, but my ticket had been deeply discounted. I didn't know it then, but the "Venus di Milo" was making her last voyage.

For the difference between the cost of sailing from Naples instead of flying, I was willing to brave the waves. Two months in Europe extended to four had exhausted my savings, and for several weeks I'd been forced to skip meals. Still, I was in no hurry to get home: I'd broken my engagement and quit my job before leaving New York. So if I stuffed myself for ten days on shipboard and metamorphosed from lean to overblown, what did it matter? There would be no one waiting to meet me at the dock.

I didn't know what the ship served upstairs in the other classes—maybe First had caviar and crêpes suzettes. Since the doors at the foot of the stairs were locked and bolted, we never saw what we were missing. On the Third Class menu, I discovered the afternoon I mounted the gangplank, sugar was the prime seduction. Sweet confections enlivened pale pasta the way desire bestirs dispirited flesh.

My engine-level cabin, I discovered, had four berths, no porthole, and five women booked in it. Two sisters from Palermo were sharing the narrow bunk above mine. In the lower berth across was a Scots lady traveling with a terrier she'd been forced to put in the luggage compartment. The occupant of the remaining upper was yet to come.

Even with four, the cabin was very crowded. I didn't even

127

try to unpack. Instead, I stowed my bags under my bunk—and escaped down a long, badly-lighted corridor lined with luggage. When I found the main stairs, I struggled up them against the crowd of arriving passengers.

It was only four o'clock, but my one meal that day had been the black coffee and two hard rolls with stringy marmalade that cheap Italian pensiones presented unvaryingly as "prima colazione." I had already signed up for the first dinner sitting, but the dining room didn't open until six.

After three flights, I saw sunlight. There, in the once-grand salon, several of the ship's minor officers were hosting a welcome reception. As the Scots lady had told me, they were serving tea.

On a podium placed before three enormous round mirrors set in blonde, scratched paneling of the 1930's style, a plump brunette in a lavender evening gown was scratching out "Arrivederci Roma" on a violin accompanied by a young man at an off-key baby grand. A waiter beckoned me across the circular dance floor to a large, curving banquette beneath an angular mosaic of a gilded Venus.

The colors of the grand salon, it appeared, had once been champagne and rose, but the heavy curtains looped to frame the portholes had aged to a dirty sand tone. At the same time, the formerly pink rug had faded to the color of a dusty brick. The banquette, perhaps originally covered in cloth that harmonized with the honey tint of the crooked paper lampshades on the branching Venetian chandeliers, had been redone in jarring white plastic.

Seated on the already-crackled cushions was a couple from Minneapolis. While we wanted for the tea and coffee the waiters were passing, we chatted. They had been on a tour, he told me, but she had become ill in Padua—a persistent, debilitating intestinal infection. They had planned to stay abroad through Christmas, she volunteered, but they were going home for Thanksgiving instead. He was in the artesian well business, he said.

When the waiter came, I took tea, loading it with sugar. The husband was maybe ten years older than I was—mid-thirties—I decided. She, perhaps because she had been ill, looked older.

The man—his name was Elwood and hers was Martha—wanted to tell me about wells, but I wouldn't listen. I had noticed that the waiters were passing trays of pastries. The pastries were small, but I boldly asked for two and got them. As if to brighten the salon's dinginess they were frosted in garish colors. One, shaped like a star, was hot yellow, and the other, a miniature mountain that reminded me of a breast, was acid green topped with a red maraschino cherry.

During the pause after the applause in which the violinist was replaced by a blonde tenor in a brown suit, Martha excused herself. I wondered if she was going to be sick.

Afterwards, in the midst of "La Donna e Mobile," Elwood asked me if I wanted the white frosted cornucopia she had left untouched on her plate. Did I? Well, I tried not to wolf it as quickly as I had the first two. As I chewed the tough, sweet pastry and swallowed the soft, yellow custard within, I felt him watching me. I wasn't sure what he was thinking, but he made me uncomfortable.

In Italy, the strangers you encountered in streets, museums, cafes were laughably obvious—breathing heavily, whispering warmly, pinching insistently. If you were involuntarily held close to them in a crowded tram or at a Papal appearance in St. Peter's Square, they took every advantage. It was constraining, maddening, but at the same time—*opera buffa*. You became furious instantly—and then forgot about it and smiled until it happened all over again.

Elwood, though, wasn't like the Italians. He was tall, pale, broad-shouldered, balding, perhaps a Swede. Although he seemed calm, even phlegmatic, there was force in his unswerving gaze. Even though he hadn't even finished his first pastry, a blue ball, I sensed that in a different way he was just as hungry as I was.

His hands were big and clumsy. I didn't like him. I didn't want to talk to him. I scraped the last smear of pastry frosting from my plate—and stood up. I nodded good-bye, and the floor fell forward beneath my feet. I took the backward sway in stride and headed for my cabin. The "Venus" had set sail.

The fifth cabin occupant was an elderly Frenchwoman who didn't speak English. Because she seemed frail and harried, I helped her bring in her bags someone had stacked outside in the corridor. She had four of them. My French is acceptable, but when she tried to thank me, I found it was impossible to make conversation over the noise of the engines without shouting.

At that point, the Scots woman came in wearing a tweed cape. Poking out underneath it from the crook of her arm was a small, grey-faced terrier. Smiling tentatively, apologetically, she tried to tell us his name. It was something like "Mr. Carouthers," but there was too much noise to be sure. Of course, the French woman didn't understand.

Because there was so little floor space, I sat on my bunk with my legs tucked under me. The Frenchwoman—her name was Mme. Vliet—objected to the dog. The Scots woman claimed stoutly in bad French that he had been trained to use the bathroom. Both women were shouting, but I stopped listening. Fully dressed, I slipped between the cold, stiff sheets. I felt the engines' rhythmic throb. Then, I slept.

I woke up ten minutes before dinner time, luckily. The cabin was empty. I combed my hair, put on lipstick, and headed down the hall to the women's toilets. As I closed the cabin door, I thought I heard a bark.

The toilets, I found out, never quite stopped flushing. If you sat on the seats, you were moistened continuously by pale green sea water gulping and churning beneath.

In the dining room, there were many Italians, some French, a few English, and only one table of Americans. Beside Elwood and Martha, it included a priest from New Orleans and a plump pair of honeymooners from Brooklyn. We introduced ourselves, but I didn't try to make conversation. Starting with the soup, then pasta, and finally, larger variants of the same pastries, I ate everything I could.

Elwood, seated at the other side of the round table, smiled at me several times during the meal. I didn't respond. After I'd polished off the last pastry, I got into a long, intense conversation with Father Francis, a Jesuit, about paintings at the Vatican. By the time we'd finished discussing Raphael vs. Michelangelo, Elwood and Martha and the honeymooners had gone. I noticed though that on the dessert plate I'd pushed aside empty, someone had placed a red, glistening cherry in the curve of my fork.

There was a weak sun as long as we were in the Mediterranean, but once we had passed Gibralter, there was no doubt it was November.

The sun rose, but it was always cloud-shrouded. The skies were continuously grey. It began to rain, and the sea roughened. Passengers no longer strolled the open decks. The only way to see the ocean's steel-colored troughs and ice-floe billows was to go to the small section of glassed-in deck and stare down through salt-stained glass while clutching one of the waist-level railings.

As the weather worsened, the rain coming in slanting sheets, the numbers in the dining room lessened. The honeymoon couple were the first to disappear. Their steward, Father Francis told me, was bringing meals to their cabin. The motion was worst when the "Venus's" accustomed, cradle-like rocking was varied by the more violent pitching from bow to stern. If the ship had ever had stabilizers, it was clear they were no longer working.

131

I had seasick pills, but they made me sleep twelve to fourteen hours a day. The giggling and coughing of the sisters in the berth above me did not disturb me; the barking of Mr. Carouthers did not rouse me. Even the steam whistle snores of Mme. Vliet, which had a guttural and distinctly foreign tone, were to me a mere lullaby. I got up for meals, of course, but even when eating I was only half-awake—which didn't stop me from stuffing myself.

One particularly rough evening (I had been helping the Scots lady minister to Mr. Carouthers, who was sicker than anyone else) Father Francis and Elwood were the only others at our table. Martha had not appeared in the dining room all day, and even Father Francis, who was ruddy and portly, was beginning to look pale.

After Father Francis excused himself, I stayed at the table, staring listlessly at the yellowing, spotted cloth as Paulo, our waiter, scraped the crumbs into a flat silver-colored dish, carefully avoiding the vase of pink plastic roses that served as our centerpiece. When he had finished, I watched the liquids in the twin cruets held in a metal frame rise and fall, rise and fall. The yellow olive oil and the red vinegar swayed with the ship— up to starboard, and then down, up to port, and then down.

The dining room was almost empty. I could see a few of the second sitting people peering through the glass doors etched with intersecting circles. I could hear music coming from the salon beyond. It was time to go, but I didn't move—and neither did Elwood. We didn't talk, we just sat.

Finally—Paulo was resetting the table—Elwood leaned toward me, his sleeve brushing mine. "Will you come into the salon with me?"

I hesitated.

"Martha's in the cabin—seasick," he told me, his breath warm against my cheek. "All she wants is to sleep."

Was there any harm in it? If there was, I couldn't picture it. That's the way it is when you're at sea day after day: the past, and particularly the future, don't seem real. I could look forward to the next meal; I could vaguely remember the last one, and the rest was sleep.

Already, I had almost forgotten my former fiancé, an artist. I had almost forgotten the dingy office where I had labored for my weekly check. I would easily forget Elwood. I would forget his artesian wells. I was not going to fall in love with him.

I heard a violin playing "Ciribirbin." Elwood stood up. He was wearing an ill-fitting blue-gray suit. He wore it every night. Perhaps it was the only one he had. He extended one of his big hands in a formal way, waiting. Without having voiced assent, I accompanied him.

In the swaying salon, a dextrous waiter was bravely passing a tray of coffee in small white cups with chipped gold rims. The violinist completed "Ciribiribin"—and then excused herself without waiting for applause. Her chin was trembling. It appeared she was going to be sick. The pianist, though, was unperturbed. After kneeling to tighten the locks on the wheels of his instrument, he launched into a medley.

Elwood sipped his coffee. I sipped mine. Then, after a pause, he leaned towards me. "Do you want to dance?"

Someone had opened one of the heavy wooden sliding doors to the deck. Cold, damp air entered in a rush. I could smell the salt, taste its harshness on the back of my tongue, feel it filling my throat. Then someone closed the door. I blew my nose. I stood up. "Yes," I told him, "why not?"

Elwood was capable of a wooden foxtrot, but when he did the waltz, which came next, it was more as if he were pacing off a well tract than essaying a dance step. Keeping his distance and sawing our intertwined hands up and down in time to the music, he traversed the virtually empty dance floor with dogged clumsiness. Finally, when it came time for a rhumba, he confronted his limitations.

"This isn't for me," he said. "Let's sit down."

So we sat facing each other across a small, round, three-

133

legged table with an ivory-colored plastic top.

"Do you want a drink?"

"I don't think so." What I did want was to go back to my berth. I had taken one of the seasick pills before eating and I craved the drug's dreamless sleep.

Because I saw Elwood wanted to order something, I agreed to a ginger ale. He took whiskey.

When the waiter in the stained white uniform returned, he brought a small, chrome dish of salted peanuts. Elwood declined; I savored them one by one. They were almost gone by the time he set down his drink and blurted: "Martha can't have children."

"Oh." I stared at him, not knowing what to say.

"She had to have a hysterectomy."

"That's too bad." The weather was rougher. The largest Venetian chandelier, the one over the dance floor, was swinging wildly.

There was a silence. I offered him the last two peanuts, but he didn't want them. I ate them and licked the salt from my fingers.

"Do you want a gelati?"

Gelati wasn't served in the dining room, at least not in third class. You had to order it extra. It wasn't cheap. It was a long time, weeks, in fact, since I'd had one. I nodded.

When the gelati came in a long stemmed, silver metal dish, it was impossibly pink—maybe raspberry, maybe cherry. The coldness made my teeth ache, but the sweetness made me smile in spite of it. Before I finished the last spoonful, the music ended. The pitching had become so violent that one of the waiters was helping the pianist chain his instrument to a pillar.

I think Elwood had finished his drink by the time his glass slid across the table and tipped onto the floor, followed by my gelati dish and spoon. After the waiter came and Elwood paid him, we got up.

In order to cross the dance floor, we had to hold onto each

other, first grasping hands, and then, when that wasn't enough, linking arms. By the time we entered the passageway to the cabins, we were clutching each other. There, even though Elwood was a big man, we were banged against one wall, then the other.

All the cabin doors were shut; there was not even a cabin boy in evidence. My cabin came before his, and as we approached the door, we were thrown, once again, against the cream-colored, fingermarked wall. Elwood, by grabbing the hand railing on either side of my waist, pinned himself against me. I don't remember that he kissed me, but he must have, for the taste of whiskey superceded the sweetness of gelati on my tongue. I do remember his mouth moving down my neck, his hands pushing my dress down my bare shoulder.

At the same time, his knee insinuated itself between mine and them rose up between my thighs, pushing and rubbing when it reached the joining. The knee was followed by a hand. His fingers, I realized, were extremely strong.

He could have done everything he wanted, I guess—I didn't have hold of anything except the lapels of his jacket—but just then I heard barking. Sure enough, the handle of my cabin door turned, and Mr. Carouthers emerged. I only caught a glimpse of his owner—she was wearing a brown plaid bathrobe, and she looked terrible—whether it was because to the sight of us or seasickness, I never found out.

In any case, Elwood released me—too quickly, it turned out, because—off balance as I was—I couldn't catch myself when the next roll came. Just as Mr. Carouthers streaked between my legs and dashed into the men's room, my head slammed full force into the opposite wall.

By the time I pulled myself together, Elwood had gone. Dazed, I made it to my cabin with the next roll. As I opened the door, Mr. Carouthers returned (had she actually trained him to use the toilet?) and slid through the opening in front of me. Falling into my berth without even bothering to examine the bruise that was rising on my forehead, I slept.

That night was the roughest of the voyage, and despite the drug, I dreamed. In the dream I was sailing First Class, but the grand salon was nothing but an enormous, white, empty room. The walls, the ceilings and the floors—as well as the tall windows to starboard and to port were bright as mirrors. The sun was everywhere.

Why was there nothing in the room? Where was the furniture? Why were there no passengers, no waiters, no musicians? I traversed the salon as if in search of something, gliding as if the floor were made of ice. I was coming from my cabin and going, perhaps, to an opulent meal in the dining room beyond. But as I crossed the room in light that was virtually blinding, I discovered that the center of the smooth, slippery floor contained a dark, circular hole. There was no guard rail, nothing to grasp, and although the swaying of the "Venus" was gentle, not violent, I was propelled, inevitably, toward the yawning opening.

I screamed as I fell, perhaps hoping that Elwood would appear from somewhere and pull me back. Instead, I plunged slowly head first, losing, rather than gaining, speed as I descended.

At the bottom—what was it? The smell in the brown darkness was like whiskey, but whatever I had fallen into was soft, sticky, sweet. Finally, as I surmounted soft billows with a stroke that resembled swimming, I realized what the substance was. I was up to my neck in pastry custard.

The next morning, for the first time, I slept through breakfast. Despite the others' comings and goings (the roughness had lessened, I heard someone say the rain had stopped) I lay almost without moving—as content and lacking in appetite as if still cradled in the custard of my dream.

Finally, I got up and went to lunch. Both Martha and Elwood were there. We were served watery chicken soup with rice and spaghetti with meat sauce, but I couldn't even finish one portion. I wasn't hungry for the usual pastries either.

I spent most of the meal chatting with Father Francis about angels, his favorite subject. His viewpoint was spiritual—he was a professor of theology. My viewpoint was corporeal—I was a student of art. Father Francis preferred the delicate and ethereal embodiments of Raphael and Perugino; I favored the full-fleshed, muscular renderings of Michelangelo. Lean or corpulent, not all angels, we agreed, had wings.

My eyes only met Elwood's once during the meal, and it was accidental: we both wanted the sugar for coffee at the same time. He looked pale and sleepy, I saw. I wondered if he too had lost his appetite. If he noticed the red bruise on my forehead, he gave no sign.

The voyage was more than half over by them, and I was getting tired of custard. At some meals, I felt so sated that I only spooned the frosting off the pastries or ate the cherry from the top. I suppose I wouldn't have done anything more than make polite dining room conversation with Father Francis and the others for the rest of the trip if the weather hadn't turned rough again on the last day out.

That evening, even Father Francis failed me. Once again, Elwood and I were the only diners at the table. We sat in silence, facing a big serving dish of pasta and a red sauce neither of us wanted. Because it was the last night, there was an extra carafe of red wine.

While I toyed with a few olives and a hard slice of bread, Elwood concentrated on the carafe. As the level of the liquid got lower, I noticed, it seemed to sway more violently with the ship.

"The other night—" Elwood essayed finally. "The other night I—"

"Don't talk about it," I said quickly, hoping he wouldn't. My bruise had healed, and I had resolved to eliminate the memory, also, from my head.

"I have to talk about it. I *can't* talk to her. You're the only one."

"I'm not at all." I paused. Paulo was clearing the dinner plates. When he had finished, he placed the familiar tray of pastries in front of us. When we were alone again, I added: "You don't even know me."

"I know you the way a man has to know a woman," he said bluntly, "—almost."

The place where the bruise had been throbbed. I was aware of the blood rushing to my face. I stared at him. I could smell the tartness of the wine on his breath. There was a red, "V"-shaped stain at the corner of his mouth. All I had to do was excuse myself, say I was unwell, go back to the cabin. But I didn't. Instead, I observed his teeth. They were large and white and regular, matching the broadness of his jaw, the firmness of his cheeks, the paleness of his slightly protruding ears.

Although the dining room was swept, irregularly by damp, icy gusts from the double wooden doors as some stalwart essayed a post-prandial stroll on the deck, Elwood appeared to be perspiring; in fact, his face glowed. There were beads of moisture on the smooth flesh above the broad arches of his eyebrows, and also, between the glistening blonde needles of the emerging beard on his chin and upper lip. In a rough hewn way, he was a good looking man.

Underneath a long damp fold of the heavy, slightly greyish table cloth, his big hand sought mine. I should have drawn away immediately, but something prevented me. The unseen grasp possessed my fingers, and then, blunt nails gently raked my palm.

"When I dig the wells," he told me, "I know what I'm doing. It's all measured out, planned in advance. With this other thing, there isn't any one thing I know to do—or way to go."

His hand had braceleted my wrist. He placed my unresisting palm on his knee, pressing it tight.

"Way to go?" I repeated stupidly, noticing that the back of my tongue was dry. There was a glass of water in front of me: it was full. But even my free hand was useless, paralyzed. The thought of raising the tumbler to my lips and draining it was appealing, pleasurable, but I lacked the will to accomplish it.

Nevertheless, my other hand was moving, propelled by the insistent pressure of his. Sliding over the soft wool fabric that shielded his leg loosely, my hand ascended over fleshed muscles until it encountered—

The ship was pitching violently. On the tray of pastries, a candied cherry detached itself from the center of a pink, frosted star and rolled over the silvered rim of the platter and onto the cloth. There, it rolled irregularly in jagged, back-and-forth patterns—leaving faint, reddish lines of indistinct calligraphy.

"S-O-*S*," exclaimed Elwood a little too loudly. Grasping a teaspoon, he rescued the cherry just as it was about to plunge into my lap.

The ship pitched perilously; I was impelled toward him. His formerly concealed hand rose to the back of my neck, and then, the hand with the spoon inserted the cherry into my unresisting mouth.

I didn't spit it out, but somehow I wasn't able to chew it either. Instead, reaching for the water tumbler with both hands—one of them moist and sticky—I raised it to my mouth. The cherry stuck in my throat momentarily, then descended. I drained the glass dry.

Even if I had been willing to succumb to Elwood, I realized afterwards, lying awake in my bunk as everyone else in the cabin slept, there was no place on the "Venus" where we could have been alone together. Either his cabin or mine was obviously impossible. Then, aware of the way the ship's pitching was forcing my shoulders, my hips to sway from side to side, I dreamily imagined embracing Elwood beside one of the ever-rushing toilets with Mr. Carouthers on guard, beneath the pi-

139

ano after midnight in the grand salon, or, frigidly, in of the ancient life boats under an icy tarpaulin.

Of course, there was no reason for me to want him at all. Elwood was married, and I felt sorry for Martha. Beyond that, what could he be to me? What did I want with Minneapolis, artesian wells—or a baby? Yet the wrongness and the impossibility did not deter me. Does one dislike pastries simply because they are neither healthful nor nourishing?

The reason I couldn't sleep was that I hungered for Elwood—not because I was going to have him, but because I wasn't. He was, he was—I was finally becoming drowsy—I couldn't think of what he was. Instead, rolling in my berth as the storm thrashed the "Venus," I envisioned the colors of the pastries amidst the shadows on the ceiling through half-closed eyes. Pink, green, golden yellow, I imagined the frostings gleaming on innumerable pastries assembled on an enormous tray. In the center, sprinkled lightly with confectioner's sugar and the thinnest possible glaze of white icing, lounged Elwood with his big hands folded—and a cherry in his mouth.

The last morning at sea was comparatively calm, but it was snowing—a wet fall that floated heavily from grey skies into grey waves. Father Francis was at the table for breakfast; so were Elwood and Martha. With Brooklyn on the horizon, even the honeymooners returned. We talked about packing. We talked about filling out customs forms. We were parting. Probably we would never see each other again.

In the confusion of disembarkation, I lost track of everyone I knew. Finally, after waiting for a taxi in the wet, sooty slush in my thin Italian shoes, I got back to the walk up apartment where I belonged.

Several hours later, just as I was struggling up the last of the flights with bags of groceries, I heard the phone ring. Before I could unlock the door, it stopped. Later when I was trying to remove the dust that had accumulated in the apartment, it rang again.

"Hello," he said formally, "this is Elwood."

"What do you want?" I blurted. I wanted to ask how he had gotten my phone number. I certainly hadn't given it to him. Could he have taken it from the unpublished passenger list?

"We're staying at a hotel, but Martha's going home at the end of the week. I'll be here a few days more, so we can get together then. I want to see you."

I don't want to see you—that's what I should have said. Instead, I simply listened with the broom in my hand. He would take me out to a gourmet dinner, he told me, nothing Italian. We would go dancing. We would "do" New York. The "Venus," did I know it, was being scrapped.

Somehow, he got me to tell him how to get to my apartment. Why I was doing it, I wasn't sure.

"I'll bring you something nice when I come." he told me just before he hung up, "something delicious."

For several days afterwards, as I made phone calls, set up job appointments, saw old friends, I retained intermittently the feeling of being at sea. In my bed alone at night particularly, it seemed I was still rocking in my narrow berth. Once, I even imagined I had heard Mr. Carouthers bark.

Perhaps because of all I had eaten on shipboard, I was seldom hungry. When a man I had known before my engagement invited me out for dinner, I left most of the meal on the plate.

As the appointed evening with Elwood approached, I grew apprehensive. Coming home early after trudging from one office to another, I took a shower, but then—couldn't decide on a dress to wear even though my appropriate choices were few.

Ten minutes before the hour, I was still in my bathrobe. Footsteps I was sure were Elwood's were mounting the stairs. Woodenly, I stood by the door, wondering what to do.

Elwood approached the door, and since there was no bell, knocked.

I didn't do anything. I just stood there with my hand on the knob.

He knocked again. I simply stood still.

When his second knock went unanswered, Elwood called my name.

"Flory—Flory."

I let him call.

"Flory, Flory, angel—"

I heard him set something down in front of the door, and then finally, I heard his slow footsteps going downstairs. Then, peering from behind the curtains at the front windows, I saw him cross the street.

Of course, the phone rang again and again until late in the evening, but I never picked it up. It wasn't until the next morning that I opened the door and saw what he had left me.

It was a large, flat bakery box with red lettering. I cut the red and white string. Inside was a cherry pie—not the kind in which the crust conceals the fruit, but the open sort in which all the cherries lie exposed and gleaming. The cherries were the brightest red.

It was only eight o'clock in the morning, but my appetite had come back to me. I ate a lot of my pie then and there. Before lunchtime, it was all gone.

There were crumbs on my cheeks, and my lips were blood red, I saw as I glimpsed myself then in the mirror. I realized though that the queasy feeling of still being aboard the "Venus" had gone. I was no longer at sea. I was about to chart a new course.

Crumbs

If you don't know how it feels to go without enough to eat for days, even weeks, you'd better not read this. Descriptions of hunger don't convey how it feels—you have to remember.

It's a while since I was 23, touring Europe alone after breaking my engagement, but I haven't forgotten. I had planned to leave from Italy anyway, but my money ran short a couple of weeks before the old liner I had booked because it was the cheapest way home was scheduled to sail from Naples. I survived, but after boarding the ship a lot thinner than I had been, I spent the whole voyage stuffing myself with pasta and custard pastries.

On the ship, a man named Elwood made overtures, but I wasn't interested. Perhaps you can only be possessed by one passion at a time. Back in New York, he came to the door of my walk-up apartment a few days later, but I wouldn't let him in. He left a beautiful cherry pie at my door.

I'd gained weight by then, and I wasn't particularly hungry, but I gobbled it up. Such passions, I guess, don't always disappear with satisfaction. Long after you're fed—or fed up—desire can consume you again and again.

After the pie I wasn't hungry—at least not that way—for a long time. Instead, another appetite consumed me and, you might say, sucked my bones. It was late November by then, and the days were short and dreary—not an auspicious time in New York. Nevertheless, even before I found a job, I met three attractive men.

Two were suitable, one wasn't. The doctor and the lawyer were introduced to me by friends. The third wasn't an Indian chief, he was Dominick. Of course, he was the one I wanted.

How did I meet him? I don't like to admit it, but it was on a street corner. I was half a block from my apartment, waiting for the light to change. I was carrying my brief case with my resume in it—on my way to a job interview.

143

It's amazing, in New York, how long you have to wait for a light. The man standing next to me—he looked older than I was, at least 30—was wearing a brown suede jacket and a red scarf. While the orange "DON'T WALK" sign was still flashing, I observed his eyes. They were a warm light brown.

He blinked. The green "WALK" sign came on. We crossed together, silent companions. When we both turned toward the avenue to wait for the light to change again, it became obvious that we were going the same way.

I was on my way to the subway, and he, he told me later, was about to eat breakfast at the corner coffee shop before going to work. He was the assistant butcher at a small neighborhood store.

Which one of us spoke first, I don't remember. I think it was he who simply said: "Dominick."

"Flory," I replied.

As formally as you could imagine, we shook hands. The only thing was—we didn't let go—we just stood there.

"What do you want?" I said finally, beginning to feel uncomfortable. It was cold, there was an icy wind, but I could feel the sweat forming on my palm.

"You." That was all he said.

Was it his eyes—or my aberration? Had the sweet, unhealthy food I had stuffed myself with on the ship affected my mind? Had Elwood's cherry pie been laced with a slow-acting aphrodisiac that—?

There was no excuse for it, none, and besides, it was out of character. My former fiancé, Popo, had been my first and only lover. I had had more than enough self respect to resist the *opera buffa* attempts of the Italian boulevardiers, and Elwood—well, he didn't count, did he?

Yet, after the handshake, I allowed Dominick's hand to lead me back across the streets we had just crossed. He lived, as it turned out, just down the block. His brownstone was similar to mine except that I was on the top floor, and he was on the first.

Willless as a dish of warm custard, I followed him inside.

"I'm married," he told me after he had shut the door. "No children yet."

I heard his words, but they seemed to have nothing more to do with me than something that might be happening at that moment back in Naples. Places and people, one assumes, continue to be more or less the same after you leave them behind. But how can you be sure of it? How does anyone know? The tub I had sailed home on, after all, was already being dismantled for scrap in Hoboken.

Besides, as if I were dizzy or even as though I were at sea again with the floor rising and falling under my feet, I was already lying on the deep crimson spread of the bed that took up almost all of the very small bedroom. As Dominick made a phone call, telling someone he would be late for work, I was staring up at the skirts of what had to be his wife's dresses. One of them, I noticed, was a bright fuscia made of several layers of chiffon. His wife, he told me later, was a hostess in a restaurant. On weekends, she liked to dance.

The encounter that followed, what can be said of it? What I remember was that, while shutting my eyes at the beginning and not opening them again until it was almost over, what I saw was the flashing traffic signs: "WALK, DON'T WALK. WALK, DON'T WALK."

Later, when I'd gone home by myself and called, belatedly, to reschedule the job appointment, I tried to put what had happened out of my mind. That was like consuming a heavy meal and then, because you were supposed to be on a diet, pretending afterwards you hadn't. You could fool other people maybe, but—stuffed to bursting—you couldn't stomach your own lie.

Maybe because I had rescheduled, maybe because I simply couldn't make myself care no matter how much I needed the salary, I didn't get the job. Even the employers who didn't cite the impracticality of my degree in art history had nothing to offer but clerical.

Afterwards, although I'd planned to stop at the store—my refrigerator was almost empty—I went straight home. There was canned soup, I remembered. It would be enough. I was tired.

Taking the long way around in order to skirt the block that contained Dominick's apartment, I got to my own building just as an icy rain began. Removing the mail from my box without looking at it, I climbed the five flights. When I got to my door, I saw a white paper package tied with white string hanging from the knob.

Once inside, I opened it. It contained two thick, pink, beautifully trimmed lamb chops of the most expensive cut packed in crushed ice. After placing them reverently in the oven to grill, I examined the mail.

On top of the pile was a postcard picturing a public library in Minneapolis. The message was short. It said: "Got home. Thinking of you, angel. Love, Elwood."

The next week, I got a job. The salary was a necessity, even though I didn't feel as needy as I had before because my dinners were augmented daily by the best cuts. It was a small, thick, prime porterhouse one night, a generous slice of salmon another. (There was a fishmonger's next door to the butcher shop, and exchanges could be arranged.) I was merely a meagerly paid receptionist and file clerk in a small private art library near Fifth Avenue, but my nightly meals were lavish, to say the least.

Fortunately, Dominick's wife (I never did find out her name) had to be at the restaurant at 7:30 in the morning, and my library didn't open until ten. So frequently, summoned by a brief phone call ("It's O.K.," was all he usually said) I visited Dominick's apartment before we both went to work.

With Popo, there had been long conversations, and sometimes, arguments. Popo was a philosophy student, a sometime painter of meticulous little landscapes, a serious person with ambitions that involved "changing things." I liked the sound of that, but we couldn't seen to agree on what those "things" were. He swore, I wept, and as time passed, we were arguing more than we were making love. Then, when our plans for the summer in Europe together were thwarted when he was offered a fellowship in Michigan, we both knew the engagement was off.

Did that mean I had to become involved with an uxorious butcher with beautiful brown eyes? It didn't, but I have to admit—reluctantly—that I was happier than I'd been with Popo. Also, although my job was almost as boring as the one I'd had before going abroad, I was free to leaf through all the art books I liked when things were slow. Happily too, the craving for sweets that had afflicted me on shipboard and after was gone: Dominick's prime cuts were pinkening my cheeks while keeping me lean.

As for our morning encounters on the bed with the crimson cover, what can I say? Shall I pretend that they were reasonable or understandable? Would it make those hours more acceptable to contend that they were punctuated by too-private-to-be-told self-revelations or that we were both seekers of deep truths?

I could say such things, I guess, or even half-convince myself—but it wasn't the case. What I craved, what I went for, was to see his eyes, t0o close to mine, and then, without thinking or talking, to simply *feel*. The pressure, the joining, the expanding of my body for his and his for mine. This was a sufficiency but never quite a surfeit: I always wanted to come back.

And did what we were doing disturb his marriage? If so, there was no sign of it. As for me, my life with the few friends I had continued undisturbed in the evenings. Sometimes I saw former classmates from college. Occasionally, I had dates that typically ended with a kiss on the cheek and a promise to call that never materialized.

At Christmas, I got a few days off to visit my parents, who were retired and lived in Florida. My father, the former head of a charitable trust, was keeping active as a deacon of a nearby church. My mother, who was younger, continued to write the series of cookbooks for which she was already known.

Of course, I didn't tell them about Dominick, and they stopped commiserating over Popo when I told them I didn't mind. "You'll find someone," my mother assured me, "a nice family man."

I nodded.

"Your own home and children," she added, "—anything else is just crumbs from under the table."

When I returned to New York with a tan, the mornings with Dominick continued, undeterred by winter. It was often cold in my apartment: there were days when the landlord claimed that something had broken down, and there was no heat at all. Dominick's building had the same problems, but his place never seemed cold to me. In the crimson bed, we made our own heat.

January, February and March were virtually a continuum. The days lengthened imperceptibly; my life went on. Finally, it began to get a bit warmer, but it appeared that nothing else was going to change. It was April before anything happened.

People pretend that in cases like that you get tired of each other. That isn't true, we didn't. The only thing I did notice was that, more and more, I began to see things inside of my closed eyelids when we were together in bed. As I've said, his eyes were special, and when I shut mine it was as if I were diving into his.

While I kept my eyes shut—even though I certainly *wasn't* asleep—I saw unremarkable things such as an old farmhouse or a small boat making its way down a calm, sunny river, things that almost seemed to be more his thought than mine. Once or twice, disturbingly, I saw dark trees from whence came a somehow-menacing child in a Prussian blue dress. Perhaps there were other visions, but I forgot them immediately. No stranger than the fact that Dominick and I barely spoke to each other, I decided, was my new-found ability to "dream" when I was awake.

One afternoon in mid-April, I decided to walk home from work. My library, in contrast to my apartment, was overheated, and I welcomed the damp, almost-spring wind that swept through the side streets from the East River. I never shopped at the market where Dominick worked—what need did I have of meat? What I did do that day though was to stroll along the opposite side of the avenue, savoring the clean look of the wooden counters, white tile walls and gleaming glass cases profusely stocked. As usual, there were prosperous-looking customers waiting. They were paying for the best, and I knew how good the best was—I was eating it.

Then, just as Dominick emerged from the back storeroom carrying what appeared to be a leg of lamb, I noticed something different about the building. As he caught sight of me, raised his arm, waved, I saw that the windows of the apartments above the store had been painted with white "X's."

I waved back. Normally I would have smiled too, but I didn't because of the sinking feeling in my stomach. There was no sign on the building yet, but I knew what the crosses meant. The next morning, after giving me a particularly long kiss, Dominick confirmed it. The building was being demolished. The shop's owner was looking for a place to relocate. So far, he hadn't found anything.

"Oh." That was all I said, but as I lay down, I noticed that the small window beside the bed, which has been shuttered all winter, was open a crack onto the drab air well. Out there, light filtered down dimly from the roof five flights up, and just below, at the bottom of the shaft, weeds were emerging between sooty piles of left-over snow. Through the screen flowed the greasy aroma of somebody's breakfast bacon, and, indefinably, the rank, disturbing smell of spring.

"I'm cold," I complained.

Dominick shut the window, pulled the shade. I put the season out of my mind. The trustees were meeting: I had to be at the library early. We only had an hour. I shut my eyes.

The next time I saw Dominick, he gave me another extra-long kiss. Then, for the first time since I had known him, we talked instead of making love. Not only was the building that contained the butcher shop being demolished, he told me, the brownstone next door, which contained the fishmonger's, was going down too. It was possible that the entire block would be demolished for a high-rise apartment complex.

Then, it was out of character—we virtually never took time to eat or drink—Dominick brewed coffee. We sat fully dressed at the kitchen table while he buttered a hard roll for each of us.

"There's more," he said finally, leaving his roll untouched. "The owner—the owner of the shop—he's found another space."

"Good—that means that—"

His eyes stopped me. "The place," he announced, looking away, "is in *Brooklyn*."

From the hard wooden kitchen chair in which I was sitting—presumably *her* chair—I could just see the corner of the bed, its crimson spread undisturbed. The color had always seemed bright to me, even lurid. I was always glad when Dominick stripped the spread back and we could lie on the sheets, which were white as angels' robes.

From a distance, the shiny spread looked darker. I knew it was red-orange, but that day it appeared alizarin—the dark, swollen color of a bruise or a wound.

"I suppose you'll be moving," I said finally.

"Have to," he said.

There was a long pause. I was still looking, at least intermittently, at the bed.

150

"It would have had to have stopped anyway," he admitted.
"Why?"

He looked away again. "My wife's quitting her job. Friday is her last day."

"She—?"

"She's expecting," he told me. "We're having a baby in August."

I looked at my watch. He looked at his. I had to be at work in thirty five minutes. There was no time to disturb the crimson cover. It was mutual. One of us—I don't remember which—knocked over an unfinished cup of coffee in haste. Then we were lying on the floor and somehow, as he drove himself against me, I slid helplessly along the polished dark green linoleum until our heads were under the table.

For the first time, I kept my eyes open through all of it. I could see the light brown coffee dripping from the table's edge. I could, as I writhed beneath him, see pale fallen crumbs from my roll on the floor beside my ear.

I was only five minutes late for work, and one of the older trustees was kind enough to tell me how well I looked.

"How do you keep those wonderful pink cheeks all through the winter?" he asked.

When I came home that night, I avoided the butcher shop. A big, juicy reminder, though, was hanging from my doorknob. I opened the package. It was the largest porterhouse I'd ever seen.

I didn't feel like inviting anyone for dinner, so I froze part of it—but not before I'd consumed all of the tenderloin and a good bit more.

As I did the dishes, I felt wonderful—physically. In my mind, though, I couldn't help remembering what my mother had said at Christmas about getting married.

That night, my bed seemed damp and cold, and I had a hard time getting to sleep. When I kept my eyes shut, I saw the green linoleum squares of Dominick's kitchen floor. Scattered across them like seeds on barren ground were the crumbs under the table my mother had talked about.

The Towers

Have you ever had an orgasm seated alone in a subway rattling through a dark tunnel with its lights flickering on and off?

No, I haven't either—that's the sort of thing you encounter in pornographic fantasy, not in real life. Yet, maybe because it's one of those March Sundays when New York makes you feel pale and nervous, stretched out, aching for sun—I do notice something as the old train bangs its way to the penultimate station.

I'm tired. I'm a 25-year old singer, and I have a new book of art songs in my lap—but I haven't opened it. My mind is somewhere else. I just sit, letting the subway throw my body around the way it's bound to do whether I resist or not.

Then, something starts inside me. Call it the clenching of a fist, or better, the pursing of a mouth for a kiss. No particular pleasure connected with it, but a release, a sense of starting again. It's what happens when you open a viewless courtyard window on a day when the ice is melting and smell the rank odor of spring and moist black earth.

I look across the aisle at my husband Jo-Jo, the composer. He is reading one of his musicology books. In fantasy, he would sense something, see from my reddened cheeks, my glazed eyes, my limp mouth that....

In reality, nothing of the kind. We are sitting separately because the car was crowded when we got on. Then, when it thinned out, neither of us bothered to move. We've been married two years, but even on the honeymoon—and before—we were never the sort of couple who has to be always holding hands, rubbing thighs, leaning against each other for mutual support. Passion—yes. Dependency—no. I've seen middle-aged couples—people of 35 or even in their forties—who just can't seem to let go of each other. We aren't like that.

The subway is slowing for our stop, but Jo-Jo doesn't even

153

look up. He is very pale, and there is a reddish purple pustule on the side of his neck. He's been working on a concerto all winter, and it's nowhere near finished. His degree is in medieval music, but his own compositions, of course, are very modern. I work part-time for a music publisher—how else could we pay for my lessons with Vidovsky out of Jo-Jo's teaching fellowship? My focus is different—*lieder*, art songs, opera. Maybe I know almost as much about music as Jo-Jo does—but not from books. What *I* know is what I hear, what I see, what I *feel*.

Then there's Robbie with his trumpet.

Want to know why I'm too sleepy to look at my songbook? It's because less than two hours ago I was pasted flat on my back on Robbie's big white bed under the skylight. The top sheet was wadded under our feet, and the bottom sheet was moist between the "V" of my limp legs. Robbie was still half on top of me, his fingers rhythmically circling the nipple of my breast, his breath coming like slow drumbeats in my ear.

I'm an adulteress. You don't have to like me, but I'm going to be honest with you. I went straight to Robbie's after telling Jo-Jo I'd be practicing at the studio. It's been that way for two months. Nights, Robbie plays trumpet in a club downtown. Afternoons, he's always glad to see me.

Robbie's bed is soft as cotton balls. It takes up most of the room, and there are no posts to anchor it. The mattress floats in the center of the floor, which is painted blue like the sea.

When I go to Robbie's we drink white wine. When we lie in bed, I see things through the old skylight upside down. Water towers poise on their cone-shaped shingle roofs, ceramic tile cornices unscroll in the wrong direction, and window flanking pilasters stand on their Corinthian capitals. When my eyes shut, it's my city. I poise on the Plaza fountain and rise to the Trump Tower. I gather garlands of stone curlicues from the Washington Square arch and then take the A-flat farewell whistle of the Staten Island ferry boat up one octave, then another.

154

In bed with Jo-Jo, I don't envision anything. Jo-Jo and I make love at night when we are both tired. I just want to get it over with and sleep. With Robbie—when we can do no more—he gives me coffee and sweet rolls. It's another breakfast. I begin the day again.

Today, I had to leave too soon. I had to tell Robbie I'd promised to be back at two to go over a medieval concert at the Cloisters with Jo-Jo.

When Robbie helped me into my coat, he was wearing his loose green bathrobe, open to the waist and beyond. He's taller than Jo-Jo and not so heavy—lithe. Bending quickly, he pulled up my skirt and kissed me down, then up.

"You're amazing," he told me. The smell of his semen was still fresh and aromatic, coming from both of us. "You have a great body. Come back soon."

I didn't have to say I'd be back. He knew.

The train bangs to a stop. It's like hitting a block of concrete or being rammed against a wall. No pleasure in it.

Jo-Jo is quick. Only one of the doors opens, but he gets through and holds it for me. I notice how white his long bony fingers are—spread on the black rubber edge of the door. The platform is cold. My shoes are the black leather pumps I always wear when I see Robbie. Robbie likes high heels. My gloves are the black, silk lined pair I got before my last audition. I should be wearing mittens and jogging shoes.

As we hurry down the platform—we're behind time because I was late getting home, you know why—I ram one of my hands into Jo-Jo's coat pocket for warmth and get an unpleasant surprise. My hand doesn't stop—it just slides down as if his thigh were a rain spout.

This must be the pocket that he has been asking me to mend for days, maybe weeks. I feel guilty. I take my hand back. My two gloves stroke each other as if they had someone else's hands in them—smoothing the wrinkles at the wrists. I think of black suede fingers caressing a white penis, rising from the base to the tip and returning to curl beneath and rise again.

The gloves are as black as Jo-Jo's hands are white. Like a marble fragment—a hand broken off at the wrist—I imagine long white fingers poised above female genitals. The middle finger settles into the center, curving into the hidden, fuchsia opening. The side fingers methodically spread the lips. I can hear the sucking sound as the rhythmic middle finger enters and withdraws, enters and withdraws.

"Hurry," Jo-Jo tells me, "the concert begins at three."

I don't want to hurry. The wine hasn't quite worn off. I'm still half asleep. Isn't adultery in books enlivening—not exhausting? You judge from your experience, but I say that isn't so. The backs of my legs ache, my neck is stiff, one of my ears is inexplicably sore. Maybe that's what guilt is—not remorse but just feeling *old*. The way I feel I could be *forty*—not 25.

At the end of the long platform there is an unpleasant surprise. When we go through the turnstiles and climb the steel steps, we discover it's *snowing*.

Snow can be like a picture postcard—dry, powdery, delightful. Not in New York. In New York, we have the other kind of snow—wet and sticky. Flowing from the north, probably the beginning of a blizzard, the snow is being carried almost parallel to the ground by the wind.

I'd promised to go to the Cloisters museum concert of medieval music—Jo-Jo's specialty. When I say I'll do a thing, I *do* it, but doing something and *wanting* to do it can be different.

"If we're late, we'll have to stand," Jo-Jo tells me.

He's right, but I'm not eager to leave the meager shelter of the subway entrance. This isn't going to be a short stroll, it's going to be a stiff, bone chilling climb. The museum modeled on medieval monasteries stands high on a wooded hill in Fort Tyron Park. If you have a car or can afford a cab, you wind in from the drive that faces the Hudson River on a cobblestoned road that goes right to the door. If you have to take the subway, you climb the steep, winding path of stone edged steps flanked by iron lamp posts. At the top, rising above the tallest trees, the precipitous entrance tower of the grey stone museum stands like a squared off obelisk.

"I don't have boots, Jo-Jo," I whine. "I don't even have a scarf." After all, I'm dressed for ardor, not ice.

Yes, I'm a loose, selfish, pleasure-loving person. I'm thin, I have a good figure, and I like to wear silky clothes and lacy underwear. When it's cold, I *feel* it. Besides, I have another audition coming up. If I should get a sore throat—

"Can't we get a taxi, Jo-Jo?" I whine again. I know we shouldn't spend the money—and won't find one anyway. The only way to approach the tower is by the steep, whitening path. Still, I like to play out my feelings— theme and variations.

"There aren't any taxis, " says Jo-Jo in a polite, patient way that is truly infuriating. "If we don't dawdle, we can make it to the top in fifteen minutes."

He steps out into the whirl of whiteness. I don't move.

"*Here*—" Awkwardly, Jo-Jo unwinds the long green scarf his mother knitted him before she died and gives it to me. Why does he have to be so *nice*? Robbie would have slapped me hard behind, made me giddy-up. Gliding his hand under my coat—maybe even feeling down the front of my skirt to see if what was always wanting him was wet—Robbie could have made me race up that hill *presto*.

Jo-Jo, who wouldn't think of doing that, is trudging toward the first steps. I'm supposed to follow. Don't I have to when I can see snow going down the back of his neck because *I* have his scarf?

When I have to do something unpleasant, I take my time. It *takes* time to feel sorry for yourself. Still, snow is sliding inside my pretty shoes. My warmth is leaving me like a flow of blood. My nipples are cold.

From the place where the steps turn back on themselves and

157

begin to be steep, Jo-Jo is calling my name. Is there an echo? Why does the echo sound like a melody?

It is colder to stay than go. I start, but walk in a way that shows I don't want to—sashaying my hips, pointing my toes. Robbie is with me, every step. I hear his horn. I see it shine, I feel it burn.

The burning of snow is different. Snow sears my eyes like needles. It spirals under my skirt like whirling knives.

Jo-Jo waits. He watches me, snow striking his face. When I am within reach, he digs into his pocket—the one that isn't torn. Silently he extracts a subway token.

I shake my head. "I *said* I'd come—even though I might rather be doing something else—"

"I can't believe that!"

"What do you mean?"

"I'm not going to argue with you. Go ahead, *have* your stolen time with Robbie—play it *rubato*! I'm too busy to join your claque—and I'm not going to be your jailer." As a gust of snow rises between us, he turns and trudges up the hill.

I watch his back retreat. I am alone on the floodlit stage of an empty theatre. I am my own audience—and I don't like the performer. He knows about Robbie. The music world is small, even in New York. Someone must have told him. Maybe he's known all along.

"Jo-Jo—"

Snow dulls sound to *pianissimo*. Maybe he hears me, maybe he doesn't. He has reached the next place where the path turns in the opposite direction.

Instead of sticking to the steps, I take a shorter route— straight up through the bushes. My soles are slipping, my heels turning, I begin to run. I run through matted branches, thick as pubic hair. They feel like barbed wire. Rising, I sever icy branch tips that break with the sound of the fracturing of small bones.

When I catch up with Jo-Jo under a great oak's arms, I am panting, crying.

"So you've decided to come."

His tone is so different from what I expect—so sad, so sympathetic. I don't know what to say. "Yes, yes—" I blurt, eager to apologize, ready to abase myself. Snow flows into my mouth like white sand.

"Then let's not stand here."

We turn toward the tower, now larger, whiter. Its shape is muted to a raised finger revealed, then obscured by clouds of snow. We still have a long way to go.

I always wear a little gold cross around my neck for luck. Now the chain has become twisted, seaming my throat. The arms of the cross prick my breasts. To untangle the chain would mean stopping, taking off the scarf, opening myself to snow. So, stiff as an icicle, I continue through deepening drifts, stepping in the hollows of Jo-Jo's footsteps. Behind us, a long way down, cars are slipping and stalling on the ice, buzzing like flies impaled on pins.

I am burning in the cold. Do I have a fever? I almost never think about death. It means nothing to me. Now, struggling to keep up with Jo-Jo, I believe cold has something to do with it. The snow, the snow.... The red pustule on Jo-Jo's neck gleams. Medieval saints, I've read, kissed lepers' sores for love of God.

We are risen. Jo-Jo is waiting for me.

"Jo-Jo," I tell him when I catch up, "I'm sorry—"

He shakes his head. "I've been pushed, busy. I should have spent more time—"

"I'll stop auditioning for a while. We'll have a baby—"

Laughter. A wet snowball hits me hard on the back of the neck. Stunned, I fall back into the snow.

Three cherubic boys come running down the mountain. They are playing in the snow, taking long, winged leaps and daring glides. Their laughter trills like flutes.

Jo-Jo is bending over me, brushing me off. "Are you hurt?"

"I don't think so—"

He pulls me to my feet and then scoops up snow with his

bare hands, sending volleys of retaliation. The cherubs fly down the mountain. Below us, they are still laughing, untouched by Jo-Jo's snowballs.

"Don't—" I beg, but he flings another barrage—and misses again.

We are at the path's last turning—almost there. We can see the high stone wall edging the road. The trouble is, the tower is crooked. The trouble is, the hill is moving.

Somewhere, there is a muted rumbling, easier to feel than hear. There may be drums buried in the hill. Because of their pounding, piles of snow are shifting, shaking.

As the snow turns, rising and then descending into softly cupped hollows, I see that there are lovers lying under the snow. Their faces are concealed, their bodies are shrouded. They are lying on black ground beneath white drifts, making love in all positions.

The snow repeats their thrustings, imitates their contortions, echoes their sighs. Their moans mingle with the wind; their ecstasy is endless. They are insatiable. The mountain, the museum and the white, trembling tower are throbbing and bobbing to the beat of their love....

Snow clouds my eyes, stones bulge beneath my feet. We are crossing the cobblestone road. We are under the tower's arch. We are in the museum. Through whitened eyelashes, I see the red brick floor of a vaulted vestibule. The tower is over our heads.

More stone steps. The long, straight flight leading to the main floor of the museum is lighted by arched windows. Getting warm is as painful as getting cold. Parts of my body seem to have separated—eyes crying, teeth aching, heart pounding, toes throbbing. I have to put the parts back together. I am not dizzy now, I am exhausted. Jo-Jo helps me.

At the top of the steps, there is a sign on a wooden stand. "Today at 3, Les Petits Chanteurs á la Montagne, Conducted by Rt. Rev. Mgr. Jacques Brumel."

We pass under a high archway into a long hall of medieval tapestries. Little boys' voices rise in an ethereal Gregorian chant and echo from damp walls of stone. Snow is falling from us, melting. We leave a wet trail.

We come to the low-ceilinged room where the Unicorn Tapestries hang. The pure white creature is pictured in seven scenes.

"...Made for marriage of Anne of Brittany to Louis XII of France in the late Fifteenth Century," Jo-Jo whispers professorially, "—sacked from a chateau during the Revolution and, for a time, used to keep potatoes from freezing."

Jo-Jo knows a lot of things like that. I stare at the tapestry in which the beautiful unicorn is surrounded by huntsmen with sharp spears. He is tormented, brutally wounded, but in the seventh tapestry, he is seated within a circular fence under a pomegranate tree amidst innumerable flowers.

"—and the unicorn was so wild and swift," Jo-Jo continues, "that neither man nor horse could overtake him. He could only be captured by a virgin, for he would meekly rest his head in her lap."

Truly, you can live with a person day after day and not know them. Why was Jo-Jo always so *calm*? So many nights, I've let him rest on my body, heard him moan in the dark, yet I don't know the answer. Why?

"The unicorn could absorb the poison of evil through his horn," Jo-Jo was explaining. "When he dipped his horn in a stream, he made the water safe for others to drink."

I imagine the stream. It is a river of melted snow silvered with shards of ice. I wonder whether Jo-Jo will go to bed with me when we go home. I am warm enough now to fantasy the heat of the embrace.

We are late, too late. The chapel where the little boys in black robes are grouped around the transept is full. An attendant says we will have to sit in the hall with the overflow.

Beside glassed-in arches facing a snow-shrouded courtyard

garden, black metal folding chairs are hastily being set up in uneven rows. We find places beside an arch with clear, diamond-shaped panes. The singing comes to us through amplifiers attached to columns with figured capitals. The sound is damp. The high voices seem to be ricocheting from the leaded glass.

The glass itself is steamy, partly because of the audience. An unexpected number has come, somehow, through the storm.

In the square garden beneath us, snow is still falling, falling. It is slanting from the north, flowing down over a stone crucifix into a circular fountain. The fountain is always being filled with snow but is never full. The wind blows the snow into one side and out the other. It is impossible to see where the snow goes.

Now I am warm, almost too warm. I am beginning to be uncomfortable. I see Jo-Jo has forgotten me again. He is absorbed in his music. Then, high above a courtyard corner, I see something the snow clouds have hidden. It is *another* tower.

Maybe tower isn't the right word. It is a flattish, two-windowed projection with a pitched roof, the kind of thing that might *suggest* a tower in an opera set. It is topped with a theatrical, ironwork ornament that seems to have sword-like edges.

It isn't right that there should be a second tower. The silly-looking thing makes me feel uneasy. I begin to fidget. I take off my shoes and rub my toes. My stockings are wet. Jo-Jo gives me a disapproving glance. I want to talk to him, but I know it will be a long time before the concert is over.

The capital of one of the columns is carved with the face of an angel. Another shows the thick body of a bear with open jaws. Rudely, I begin to hum one of the songs I like to sing.

Jo-Jo gives me another look. "What's wrong with you?"

I shake my head. "Nothing." That's a lie. I can't explain why, but I don't like the way the ethereal chanting is winding around us—ropes of sugar. I don't like the steamy, enclosed warmth of the hall, either. It is like being imprisoned in a glass jar.

In this sweaty, enforced silence, the snow is beginning to appeal to me. I imagine the openness of the far side of the museum that faces the river. I imagine the gliding ease of descending the hill we climbed. Like the cherubs, we will fly. Surreptitiously hoping he won't notice, I take Jo-Jo's scarf out of my coat pocket.

He does notice, but I am thinking of the unicorn and his blood-dripping wounds. As I push my chair back, the metal legs grate along the floor. Jo-Jo gets angry. He doesn't like to have his music interrupted. Other people are looking at me.

"I'll meet you outside," I tell him in normal tones—no *sotto voce*. I stand up.

Maybe he thinks I have to go to the bathroom. Whatever he thinks, he doesn't stop me. I suppose he thinks I'll be waiting beyond the hall of the unicorn tapestries. I know I won't.

It so happens that I like things definite. What I sing has verses and choruses, refrains and resolutions. Jo-Jo's music— yes, it *is* beautiful—just goes on forever. No one can wait forever.

I go out the same way we came in—down the long stair to the vaulted vestibule, through the oak door. Snow is still falling.

In a few minutes, I'll be going home with Jo-Jo. By then, the snow will be deeper, the sun lower, the wind harsher. I'll do whatever he wants when I get home, won't I? For now though, I need just a few minutes to find out why there are two towers instead of one. Why does the big tower—so square and thick and dignified with its balanced rows of arched windows— have to be balanced by a *little* one that looks (I can see it now as I follow the white path that curves around the building) completely ridiculous, unconvincing?

Then—I am climbing through the drifts to the square courtyard garden—the question ceases to interest me. I am beneath the clear, leaded glass windows beside which we were sitting.

163

The concert is over, I can see people filing from the hall.

By chance, Jo-Jo is passing one of the windows above me. His head is down, he is abstracted, still caught up in the music. Then—I can't help myself—I make a big soft snowball and launch it at the panes. He is putting on his overcoat. He turns, he sees me.

I read on his face all the things that he would say to me if I could hear him. "What are you doing down there? Why did you leave the concert?"

For the first time all day, I have his full attention. So playfully taking advantage, I spread my arms like a diva. The snow is flowing into my face from the towers, both of them. Still, I open my mouth. I begin to sing.

Jo-Jo looks concerned. He frowns. That encourages me. I launch into my repertoire. First, "La Donna e Mobile," then, "Sempre Libera." Finally, getting carried away, I essay one I don't know well, "The Song of the Willow" from *Otello*. As Vidovsky says, I still have things to learn about control and breathing. Still, I don't hold back. When I sing, I *sing*.

When I finish, I bow and curtsy. Maybe other people see me, maybe they don't, but Jo-Jo is transfixed. He is standing close to the glass with his mouth open. He has raised his palms and pressed them against the panes.

I am in my glory. I smile, I smile, I throw him kisses as if he were an enormous claque. It is the end of the act, but I am prepared for encores. To Jo-Jo the amazed, to Jo-Jo the unbelieving, I am ready to give it all back.

Bending forward, I gather snow like bouquets tossed from Dress Circle boxes. I toss it up against the glass. But the snow is light, lighter than roses. Some sticks, but a lot comes back against me—on my head, on my shoulders.

I am wound up like Olympia in *Tales of Hoffman*. I do not stop, and I have gathered so much snow, hurled so much against the panes, had so much fall back upon me that I can't see Jo-Jo. Is he on his way to get me?

164

Then, through one diamond-shaped pane. I see his face. Roughly carved as a crucifix, it is crimson with pain.

I am cold again, even colder than before. My voice is faltering, my knees bending. My gold chain is a circle of ice at my throat. Still, still as if summoned by a far away trumpet, I keep singing. If there is anything stronger than snow, believe me, *mio caro, mia cara*, it is a song, *yes*, a song.

The Nurse

The front door shut with soft finality. The nurse was gone. She was not coming back. At last the mother had the baby to herself.

The baby, a three-week-old girl, was sleeping in her bassinet. The bassinet, left in the attic by people who had once owned the house and repainted by the father, had a white nylon cover dotted with blue tulips. It was edged with lace, and small bunches of pink, artificial flowers had been attached with pink ribbons at the head and foot. The lace and the flowers had been added by the mother. Pink was a concession to chance; lace was the mother's concession to sentiment.

Opening a trunk a month before the baby came, the mother had discovered an ancient, hand-sewn christening dress pinned to a note neatly penciled by her great-grandmother. "This little dress was made for Libbie the winter before her birth. Every stitch my own." The note had made the mother feel warm and soft. The great-grandmother had been gone for half a century, but the mother shared her loving anticipation of a child. A person who never sewed if she could help it, she had spent an entire evening hand stitching lace to the bassinet cover.

Older than most for a first child, the mother considered herself a pragmatist. She made plans ahead—that was where the nurse came in. The nurse had been hired in advance through an agency. The husband had gone to interview her. The nurse had telephoned the mother several times. From beforehand the relationship seemed set. A sympathetic German lady, the nurse would be warm and helpful. "I don't know anything about babies," the mother confessed to the nurse on the phone, "you'll have to show me."

The Sunday of going home from the hospital was vague afterwards in the mother's mind. All the hospital days had been alike—pink walls, pink roses—the joy of the baby and the gentle uncertainties of the first nursings merging with the soft, prematurely warm spring weather, moist grey skies and light green leaves. The husband took the mother and the baby home from the hospital at eleven. The nurse was to arrive at three. To avoid waking her husband with the night feedings, the mother settled into the best spare room. She went to bed with the bassinet wheeled as close as possible. She was weak but happy. The nurse, she fantasied, would complete the picture. The mother had already written out a desirable feeding schedule with notes on what the nurse would do. It was all planned, she believed, lingering pleasantly between sleep and waking, all organized in advance.

Then the nurse came.

The mother awoke to see a thin, white-haired woman standing at the doorway smiling. The nurse wore white and was of a pleasantly appropriate age—somewhere near sixty, the mother guessed. The baby woke up and began to cry, and the nurse picked her up. She made approving noises to the baby and called her a German name the mother did not understand. The mother saw only the back of the baby's head.

"She has a lot of hair—" the mother said to the nurse. The mother was particularly proud of the baby's thick, straight hair. Many other babies in the hospital had had little or no hair. The mother had no particular dreams or ambitions for her child, but she took the hair as a mark of distinction. Her first glimpse of her child had been of the dark crown of her head, and later, at hospital feeding times, the mother would lie with the door of her room open, listening lovingly for the high-pitched cries that counterpointed against the creaking of wheels as the iron cribs were brought sown from the nursery, and finally get up and peer into the hall to single our her daughter by the forest of hair that sprouted from the child's head.

The nurse praised the child's hair, and the mother took it as a sign of friendship and understanding. The nurse took the baby away to change her, and the mother fell into an exhausted sleep. When she awoke, the baby was gone. Someone had wheeled the bassinet from the room and she had not even heard it go. She got up and found the nurse in the next room. The bassinet was standing beside the nurse's bed, and in it the baby was asleep.

"You took her?" the mother demanded, sleepy and uncertain.

"It is always done that way," the nurse explained. "The baby sleeps in the nurse's room—then I can take care of her at night and you can rest."

The mother wanted to argue, but as she hesitated in the doorway, she felt the familiar stab of pain. She retreated to the bathroom for one of the doctor's pills and then returned to her bed. Did the nurse know best after all? Instinct denied it, but before she could reach a conclusion, she slept again.

When the nurse brought the baby in to feed, the mother did not bring up the question, but afterwards, when the baby had finished nursing, the mother resisted the nurse's first effort to take the baby away.

"Let her stay here," she told the other woman, guarding the baby who was now snoring very softly in the circle of her arms.

The nurse shook her head, pursed her lips. "It isn't wise—" the nurse began.

"But I'm not going to sleep," the mother said, "I just want to hold her."

Still disapproving, the nurse withdrew. She would not go too far, the mother felt. A line had been drawn. The mother relaxed. The child lay in her arms like a jewel in a simple setting. The mother thought of the years she had wanted the child. Outside, the sun was sliding down behind the white clapboard house across the street. The room was on the ground floor, and the mother could see a green broad-leafed weed starting under the window....

Had she slept? The mother opened her eyes with a start of fear. The child still breathed peacefully in a nest of covers, cradled between the arm and the breast. But the mother's eyes measured the long drop from the bed to the floor, saw that if the covers had gone only a few inches higher they would have come over the child's nose. She had read of mothers who had rolled over on their babies in bed and smothered them. For a moment, she lost faith in herself. Lifting the baby carefully, she took her into the nurse's room.

During the first days, the mother and the nurse often chatted while the baby was nursing. The nurse was a refugee; she had left Germany in the Thirties, escaping to Holland before coming to America. The nurse had seen much of Europe in her youth and had warm recollections of spas and seaside resorts, old-style hotels and sidewalk cafes. She still spent vacations abroad. The mother also traveled, and because of the bond she considered the nurse a cultivated person. If she had given over her child and her house to the care of the nurse, she could at least reassure herself that they were in understanding hands. Besides, there was no choice; she was too tired to do otherwise. Between nursings, the mother slept, ate, slept again. The baby fed every four hours—day merged into night and then to day with little differentiation.

After several days, it developed that the nurse wanted the room in which the mother was sleeping. It was the larger and lighter of the two. The nurse's room was damp, she said. The room was small and dark, and the way the bed was pushed in a corner was "not nice."

At first, the mother resisted. She wanted the room she was in—not for aesthetic reasons but because the bed had a headboard which she could lean against while nursing. The other bed had none and would slide away from the wall. But soon the subject of the room became paramount—crowding out the conversations about Europe at nursing times—until the mother nearly forgot the baby at the breast—so much had the nurse come to occupy her thoughts.

Finally, the mother gave in. The time of exchanging rooms

came and was more difficult than she had expected. There were items in the first room, it developed, that the nurse still wanted—a bedspread, a blanket, a certain chair. There were a number of things in the house, it seemed, that the nurse considered "not nice."

When it was all over, the mother lay in the bed without the headboard and did not move. She was too exhausted to sleep. When the nurse brought the baby in to feed, she saw how the mother felt and became quiet. "You have the baby this way," she said, after watching for a while in silence, "I have her only to change her after she has eaten." It was said half in apology, half in self-defense.

Later, as she was falling asleep, the mother saw that she, the mother, still had far more in the nurse's eyes despite the lesser room. For what the nurse wanted was not the room but the baby.

In the middle of the second week, the nurse took her first day off. She left when the baby was sleeping. The baby was fine all afternoon, nursing well and falling asleep easily when she was flushed and satisfied. The first time the mother changed the baby, she realized that she had never seen the child entirely naked before. Then that night the mother saw that she perhaps did not know the baby at all.

The mother nursed the baby at ten as usual and then, shortly after eleven, went to bed herself. Scarcely had she turned out the light when the baby began to cry. The baby cried steadily until after two in the morning. The mother tried everything. She changed the baby, rocked the baby, sang to the baby. She nursed the baby until she was certain there was no milk left. She became so tired that she no longer thought of the baby as a baby at all. The baby was a voice box with a few attachments. She did not lose patience, but she lost contact. No longer the bud of a sensible adult individual, the baby was an impersonal and unanswerable force.

It took the mother two days to recover from the nurse's day and night off. She dragged with fatigue and her milk was scanty. "Now give her enough—" the nurse told the mother each time she brought the baby in to feed, somehow suggesting that the mother would have willingly deprived the baby. The mother did not answer the nurse, but she had begun to count the days until the three weeks would be over and the nurse would go for good.

By the end of the second week, the nurse had things in the house almost as she wanted them. The mother had stopped trying to prevent the nurse from waking the baby early for the two p.m. feeding so that she, the nurse, would be free to watch a favorite TV serial that began at one-thirty. The nurse "suggested" what the mother might order from the store, and when something was lacking that the nurse wanted—white bread, for instance—the nurse ate four slices of white bread a day— the nurse won her point by offering to pay for it.

During a succession of cool, rainy days, the nurse kept the heat in the house so high that both the mother and the husband were flushed and itchy. The nurse said the heat was for the baby, but to the mother the baby seemed more fretful—perhaps feeling the warmth as much as she was.

When the phone rang, it was often for the nurse. Some days, the nurse received two or three calls. Her son called; the lady with whom she shared an apartment called; other friends who were also baby nurses called. Mother's Day was coming, and the nurse was hoping her daughter-in-law would invite her for dinner. When the mother summoned the nurse to the phone, the nurse came eagerly, ringed with smiles, and the mother felt as if she, not the nurse, had been the one hired to work in the house.

But just as surely as the nurse's influence peaked, it had to decline. The mother was growing stronger. On the Monday of the third week, the mother spoke sharply to the nurse when she woke her from a nap unnecessarily. (The nurse was always waking the mother for things that did not matter—to ask where something was or tell her an insignificant thing about the baby.) The next day, the mother went out to the hairdresser for the first time. It was only for two hours, and she had looked forward to it. She nursed the baby just before leaving and left with a clear conscience. Instead of taking the shortest route, she drove through the center of town, looking at shop windows and people on the streets like a person returned from afar. Amidst the small, steady flow of activity, the baby seemed less awesome and important. At the same time, the mother saw adults passing by from a new perspective. All, she mused, had been b abies once. Had the fat man entering the hardware store once been a feeding problem? Was the red-lipped woman coming from the drug store a former victim of thrush? Even Napoleon could have had cradle cap, and perhaps tomorrow's potentate was now crying irritably from diaper rash. The idea made the mother smile. She felt better, she decided—much better.

When the mother still had ten minutes more to stay under the dryer, the nurse called. The baby had been crying for forty minutes, she said, when was the mother coming home? The mother explained that she would be at least half an hour. Couldn't the nurse quiet the baby?

The mother left the hairdresser's as quickly as she could. As she got into the car she struggled with herself. It was long past lunchtime and she was starving. Clearly she would have to nurse the baby as soon as she got home, and the nurse would not give her time to eat. Guiltily, she turned the car in the opposite direction from the house and drove a mile out of the way to a hamburger stand. She got food to take out and drove back home as fast as she could. When she got there, the baby was asleep.

The mother exploded. Why couldn't the nurse do her own job? Why was she always calling the mother, waking her, demanding things? The nurse defended herself at first, but the mother kept on. If the nurse didn't like it, she could <u>leave</u>, she told her. Then the mother went to her room and shut the door. For a moment she stood before the mirror, admiring the way her hair looked, then she realized how tired she was and lay down.

The mother was awakened by the nurse tapping at the door. The nurse had the baby in her arms, and the baby was crying to be fed. It was raining and the room had grown dark. A pile of books on the table had obstructed the clock, and the mother felt confused—as if a long time had passed without her realizing it.

The nurse did not stay in the room while the mother fed the baby, but she left the door open. The mother saw her moving in the hall, saw the nurse bending to straighten the corner of the rug as a woman might in her own home. The mother saw that she had slept less than an hour. She was still tired. She knew that she would not tell the nurse to go because there were only three days left of the time agreed upon. She sensed that the nurse knew it too. The mother was still too weak for a full-scale fight. Since her own victory was merely a matter of time, she saw no reason to rush to an unnecessary and exhausting engagement.

On the last day, the nurse spent most of the afternoon in the living room with the baby while the mother rested. When the nurse came to put her things in the vestibule where it would be easy for the taxi man to get them, the mother came out and they chatted amicably. In the last half hour, while the nurse waited for the taxi, it was as it had been in the beginning. The nurse sat comfortably in the mother's room and they discussed European resorts. The nurse talked of the late Twenties in Germany. "That was my best time," she told the mother. "After my son was born I had a baby nurse myself—it was another life. I tell people I've had three lives—one here—one there—and—"

The baby was crying. The mother went to the living room

to take the baby from her carriage. When she returned with the baby in her arms, the nurse's face grew tight and wan. "Oh—" she said softly, looking at the baby quickly and then looking away, "—I had said good-bye to her in there—"

"I'll send you a picture," the mother promised, "I'm going to get one taken when—"

The taxi was honking in the driveway. The mother put the baby in the bassinet and went to help the nurse with her luggage. She saw she would never learn what the nurse's third life had been. Perhaps, she thought as she opened the front door, she had scarcely known the nurse at all.

"My daughter-in-law has invited me for Mother's Day," the nurse told the mother as they were saying good-bye.

"I'm glad," the mother said, really meaning it.

Afterwards the mother found herself sitting in the nurse's room facing the broad-leafed weed outside the window. It had grown at least a foot since the mother had slept in the room.

The baby had gone back to sleep in the bassinet, but the mother kept getting up to look at her. Still thinking of the nurse, she saw that she too would lose the baby eventually—not to another nurse—but because the baby would no longer be a baby. However, that was like all the natural separations of life— inevitable as the withering of a leaf from a branch. One said good-bye to first love, first youth, children—and eventually, to life itself. Still, the important thing was the moment—*this* summer—*this* child. When the time came, she like the nurse would have to relinquish—but the time had not come.

The nurse was gone. Nothing came back. The baby was crying again. The mother felt herself filling with milk. Happy with anticipation, she went to the crying child.

ABOUT THE AUTHOR

A fiction writer, poet, critic and graphic artist, Elisabeth Stevens is the author of nine books. Her collections of short fiction are *Cherry Pie and Other Stories*, Lite Circle Books, 2001; *In Foreign Parts: Nine Stories*, Birch Book Press, 1997; *Horse & Cart: Stories from the Country*, Wineberry Press, 1990; and *Fire & Water: Six Stories*, Perivale Press, 1983. Her poetry books are *Household Words*, Three Conditions Press, 2000; *The Night Lover*, Birch Brook Press, 1995; and *Children of Dust: Portraits and Preludes*, The New Poets Series, 1983. Also, *Elisabeth Stevens' Guide to Baltimore's Inner Harbor* was published by Stemmer House in 1981, and in 2000 Goss Press published *Eranos*, a limited edition book-in-a-box consisting of the author's short story and her five original copperplate etchings.

Stevens is the winner of six fiction awards, two from *The Maryland Poetry Review* and four from *Lite: Baltimore's Literary Newspaper*. Her one act play "I Told You So" received an award from the Baltimore Writers Alliance, was read at the Fells Point Corner Theatre in Baltimore and at The Writers Center in Washington, D.C. and was produced at Notre Dame College of Maryland.

Her etchings have been shown at Atelier A/E and Stephen Glang Gallery in New York City, at Government House in Annapolis, at The Corcoran Gallery in Washington, D.C., at the University of Minnesota, and at the Venice Art Center and the Fort Meyers Alliance for Arts in Florida. Her first one person exhibition was at Notre Dame College of Maryland in 1997; her second was at Galerie Francoise in Baltimore in 2000.

She is a former art critic of *The Washington Post*, *The Wall Street Journal*, *The Trenton Times* and most recently, *The Baltimore Sun*.

Cherry Pie ⸺